Meg's Fri

A Story for Girls

Alice Corkran

Alpha Editions

This edition published in 2022

ISBN : 9789356894921

Design and Setting By
Alpha Editions
www.alphaedis.com
Email - info@alphaedis.com

Contents

CHAPTER I.

MEG.

It was a queer old house in Bloomsbury, that had been fashionable some two hundred years ago, and had fallen into abject neglect. The hall door was dim for want of paint, and weatherbeaten to a dirty gray; the lower windows were tawdry with vulgar blinds and curtains, and enlivened with green boxes full of a few pining flowers. The drawing-room windows showed a sort of mildewed finery, and then, in melancholy degrees, poverty claimed the upper stories. It had all the features and cast of a London lodging house.

Within, the house carried out the same suggestion of past grandeur and present decay. The hall was wide, dingy, and unfurnished; the staircase of oak was impressive, stained, and dusty.

On the topmost step of the top flight might habitually be seen, toward sunset, a child seated and watching, with head thrust through the banisters. She would sit still until there came the scrape of a latchkey turning in the lock, and the sound of footsteps in the hall. Then the mute little figure would grow full of sudden life; the little feet would run down faster than eye could mark. Arrived in the hall, the child would stop with sudden dignity before a man, robust and tall, and looking up, ever so high, into a bright, young, manly face smiling down upon her, she would lift her tiny forefinger, and some such colloquy would ensue:

"You are late; where have you been, Mr. Standish?"

"At work, Meg—at work all the time."

"You have not been to the parlor of the Dragon?"

"No, Meg; not set my foot inside it."

"You have not been with those horrid whisky-smelling men?"

"Not seen one of them, Meg."

"Then you may come up," the child would say, taking his hand and leading him up.

Mr. William Standish was beginning life as a journalist. He contributed descriptive articles to a London paper, and was correspondent to a colonial journal. His straight-featured countenance expressed energy and decision; his glance betokened a faculty of humorous and rapid observation; closely cropped blond hair covered his shapely head.

The journalist occupied the rooms on the upper story of Mrs. Browne's lodging-house. He was the single member of the nomadic population sheltering under that decaying roof who lived among his household gods. He had made it a stipulation, on taking the rooms, that he should have them unfurnished, and he had banished every trace of the landlady's belongings.

The child was Meg. She went by no other name. When Mrs. Browne answered her lodgers' queries concerning her, she replied vaguely that the child had been left in her charge. Meg went to an over-crowded school in the morning, and did odd jobs of household work in the afternoon. In the intervals she sat on the topmost stair, watching the social eddies of the shabby miniature world breaking down below. She was a silent child, with a mop of dark brown hair and gray eyes, the gaze of which was so sustained as not to be always pleasant to meet. The gravity of her look was apt to make those upon whom it was directed feel foolish. She repelled the patronizing advances of lodgers, and, when compelled to answer, chilled conversation by the appalling straightforwardness of her monosyllabic replies.

Two events had influenced her childhood. One day, when she was about seven years of age, she had suddenly asked the old servant, who from time immemorial had been the sole assistant of Mrs. Browne in discharging her duties toward her lodgers:

"Tilly, had you a mammy?"

"Lor' bless the child!" answered Tilly, almost losing hold of the plate she was washing. "Of course I had."

"Has every child got a mammy?" persisted Meg, with deliberate plainness of speech.

"Of course they have," answered the old woman, utterly bewildered.

"Is madam my mammy?" asked the child, a slight tremor perceptible in the slower and deeper intonation of her voice.

"Madam" was the name by which she had been taught to call Mrs. Browne.

"No!" answered Tilly sharply; "and if you ask any more questions ye'll be put into the dark closet."

The threat, that brought to the child's mind associations of terror, wrought the desired effect of silence. She stood, with her glance unflinchingly directed on Tilly's face, and with a question trembling on her lips, until the old servant turned away and left the kitchen.

Hitherto Meg had never asked a question concerning herself. She had accepted a childhood without kissings and pettings—a snubbed, ignored childhood—with a child's sainted powers of patience and resignation.

That night, as the old woman was composing herself to sleep in the attic that she shared with the child, she was startled by Meg's voice sounding close to her ear, and, turning, she saw the diminutive figure standing near her bed in the moonlight.

"Tilly," she said, "I don't mind your locking me up in the dark closet, if you'll just tell me—is my mammy dead?"

"Yes," said Tilly, taken off her guard.

There was a moment's pause, and an audible sigh.

"I'll never be naughty again, Tilly—never," resumed the child's voice, "if you'll just tell me—what was she like?"

"You'll not ask another question if I tell ye?" replied Tilly after a moment of silent self-debate.

"No, Tilly."

"Never another? Do ye hear?"

"Never, Tilly," repeated the child solemnly.

"And you'll never let madam know as I told you?" said Tilly excitedly, sitting up in her bed.

"Never."

"Then, I don't mind saying, for I thinks as you ought to know, as she was as pretty as a picture as I ever saw, and the gentlest, sweetest, ladiest lady," said Tilly, nodding, as a sharp sob sounded in her throat.

"Lady?" said Meg.

"A lady she was in all her ways, every bit of her; and the man as let her die here all alone was a brute—that he was!" said Tilly, with vehemence.

"What man?" asked the child, in a low voice.

"Go to bed," said Tilly severely, through her sobs.

"Was it my pappy?" said the child, who had seen and heard strange things during her seven-years' life.

"Go to bed," repeated Tilly. "You promised as you'd never ask another question."

"I will not, Tilly," said Meg, turning away, and returning through the moonlight to bed.

The child kept her word, and never alluded to the subject again to Tilly.

A few days later, when she was helping the old servant to tidy the rooms after the departure of some lodgers from the drawing-room floor, Tilly was surprised by the eagerness with which she craved permission to keep a crumpled fashion-plate that she had found among the litter. It represented a simpering young woman in a white ball dress, decked with roses. Permission having been granted her to appropriate the work of art, Meg carried it up to her attic, and hid it away in a box. Had any one cared to observe the child, it would have been remarked that she, who kissed nobody, lavished kisses upon this meaningless creation of a dressmakers' brain; gazed at it, murmured to it, hid it away, and slept with it under her pillow.

The next great event marking Meg's childhood had been the arrival of Mr. William Standish to the lodging-house. It had occurred nearly two years after the talk with Tilly concerning her mother. Meanwhile the old servant had died.

Meg had watched with interest the arrival of the new lodger's properties; and she had listened, fascinated, to his lusty voice, singing to the accompaniment of hammering, and rising above the flurry of settling down.

On the third evening Mr. Standish, who had observed the little figure cowering in the dusk, and had once or twice given to it a friendly nod, invited her to enter. Meg held back a moment, then shyly walked in.

She had a general impression of books and writing materials, pipes, and prints on all sides, and of an atmosphere impregnated with the perfume of tobacco.

After another pause of smileless hesitation, she took the footstool her host drew for her by the fire. At his invitation she told him her name, and gave a succinct account of her general mode of life. She admitted, with monosyllabic brevity, that she liked to hear him sing, and that it would please her if he would sing for her now. She sat entranced and forgetful of her surroundings as he warbled:

"Nellie was a lady—
Last night she died,"

and followed the negro ballad with a spirited rendering of the "Erl King."

At his invitation she renewed her visits. She was tremendously impressed when he told her that he wrote for the papers; and was dumb with amazement when he showed her, in a newspaper, the printed columns of which he was the author.

They had been acquainted about a week, when Meg broke the silence set upon her lips, and spoke to her new friend as she had never spoken to human being before.

Mr. Standish had recited for her the ballad of the ghostly mother who nightly comes to visit the children she has left on earth, and till cock-crow rocks the cradle of her sleeping baby. The young man was astonished at the expression of the child. Her cheeks were pale; she breathed hard; her round opened eyes were fixed upon him.

"I wish mother would come just like that to me," she said abruptly.

"Your mother—is she dead?" he asked gently.

She nodded. "She's dead. I never saw her—never. I'd love to see her just a-coming and standing by my bed. I'd not be a bit frightened."

"But if you have never seen her you would not know she was your mother," he replied, impressed by the passionate assertion of her manner.

"Oh, I'd know her! I'd know her!" said the child, with vivid assurance. "Soon as she'd come in I'd know her. She was a lady."

"A lady!" he repeated. "How do you know? What do you mean?"

"Tilly told me. Tilly's dead," answered Meg with ardor. "She told it to me once before; and I went to see her at the hospital, and she said it again. She said, 'Meg, your mother was a lady—the sweetest, prettiest, ladiest lady'—that's what she said; 'and, Meg, be good for her sake.'" She paused, her eyes continuing to hold his with excited conviction. "That's how I know she was a lady," Meg resumed; "and I know what a lady is. The Misses Grantums down there"—infusing scorn into her voice as she pointed to the floor to indicate she meant lodgers who lived below—"they're not ladies though they've fine dresses; but they have loud voices, and they scold. I go to the corners of the streets. I watch the carriages. I see the ladies in them; and when I see one gentle and a-smiling like an angel, I say mother was like one of these. That's how I'd know what she'd be like. And," she added more slowly, lowering her voice to a confidential whisper and advancing a step, "I have a picture of her. Would you like to see it?"

"I would," he answered, thinking that at last he was approaching a clew to the mystery.

She dashed off, and in a moment returned with something carefully wrapped up in tissue paper, and gently drew out a limp picture, that she held out at arm's length before the young man, keeping it out of his reach.

"There, I'm sure she'd be like that—all smiling, you see. And those beautiful curls, are they not lovely? and those large eyes and those roses? I'm sure she'd be just like that."

"But let me hold it—just with my finger tips," he pleaded, as the child jealously held the print away from him.

She slowly relinquished it to him and stood at his elbow.

"That's a picture taken out of a book—not a portrait," he said.

"I picked it up. Some lodgers had gone away. I found it in a corner. Isn't it lovely? I'm sure she'd be just like that," reiterated Meg.

Mr. Standish was silent a moment. He was moved, yet he felt impelled to speak words of wisdom to the child. Mooning about corners of streets watching ladies drive past, and nursing those queer, foolish, ambitious ideas about her mother was not likely to lead to any good. He thought the whole story was probably without a grain of truth, the absurd fabrication of some old woman's brain, and likely to prove hurtful to Meg in giving her false notions concerning her duties in life.

He paused, revolving his words, anxious not to hurt, yet deeming it incumbent upon him to expel this foolish fancy.

"My dear child," he said at last, "why do you imagine your mother was like that picture, or like one of those ladies in the carriages? For all you know they may be lazy, vain, and selfish. It is not the pretty dress that makes the lady, or the face either. Is it not far better and more reasonable to think of that dear mother, whom you never saw, as one of God's own ladies? These ladies are found in all sorts of conditions, sometimes in caps and aprons, sometimes in beautiful bonnets, very often with brave, rough hands. What is wanted to make a lady is a kind, honest heart."

"No, that's not being a lady," interrupted the child, with a flash and a toss of her head. She spoke with decision; but her voice faltered as if she had received a shock. Taking the picture from the young man's hand, she began carefully, and with a trembling elaborateness, to replace it in its coverings. "Jessie's good, and so was Tilly. They work hard, and scrub, and run about on errands. They're not ladies. A lady's quite different," continued Meg, suddenly facing him and speaking with vehemence and clearness. "She's rich, and never scolds or cheats. She does not work at all—not a bit; people work for her and drive her about, but she does nothing herself. She has never dirty hands, or her cap all untidy, or looking all in a fuss. She does nothing but smile and look beautiful, like an angel," concluded Meg triumphantly, reiterating her favorite simile.

"Meg," said the young fellow, seeing more clearly the necessity to root out this absurd ideal from the child's mind, "you are talking very foolishly. A lady is, indeed, not necessarily an angel. You say a lady must be rich. Now, if your mother was rich, why are you poor? Would she not have left you her money in dying, and you would have been rich like her?"

"I don't know anything about that," said the child, growing a little pale, and beginning once more to fidget with the fashion-plate.

"It is for your good, Meg, that I speak," resumed the young man. "You must wish to be like your mother; and you cannot grow up good and hard-working and honest if you think your mother was rich and left you poor, with no one to look after you or care for you."

"It was not her fault," said the child faintly.

"It would have been her fault," he answered severely, shaking his head. "My dear Meg, put away this foolish idea. Call up your mother to your mind as a good, toiling woman; one of God's ladies, as I called her before. Try to be like her. Lay aside the thought that she was one of those carriage ladies."

"I won't!" interrupted the child, standing pale and upright, clutching the fashion-plate close up against her chest. "It's a lie! She was a lady!"

A smothered exclamation rose to Mr. Standish's lips. It was the first offensive word he had heard the child use.

"Meg," he cried, following the fluttering little figure up the stairs.

He saw her enter an attic; he heard the door slam and the bolt drawn.

"Meg," he called again gently.

There came no answer; but Mr. Standish thought he heard the sound of passionate sobbing. He waited, called a third time, and receiving no response he shrugged his shoulders and turned away.

The exigencies of the press absorbed Mr. Standish so completely that for the next few days he had no time to think of Meg. He noticed that the corner on the top lobby was empty, and a vague feeling of regret crossed his mind.

On the third day he was disturbed by a great clatter in the kitchen and the noise of many voices, above which that of Meg rose shrill and angry. Jessie, the hard-worked slavey of the establishment, admitted when she came up with the coal-scuttle, in answer to Mr. Standish's inquiries concerning the cause of the trouble, that it was Meg's fault. She was not like the same child. She was like beside herself—she was—these last three days.

Mr. Standish was perplexed, and resolved, after completing the weekly budget he was writing for the *Melbourne Banner*, to seek out the child, and get the clew to this sudden demoralization.

He was confirmed in this resolution when, in returning from the post, he came upon Meg in fierce encounter with some boys. She was fighting valiantly, but numbers proved too much. Mr. Standish stepped up to the rescue. He caught one boy by the ear, rolled another in the dust, and generally dispersed the assailants on all sides. Meg waited, watching, on the outskirts of the fray; but as soon as Mr. Standish had disposed of her enemies she turned and fled, disheveled, homeward. The account her rescuer received left little doubt on his mind that Meg had been the aggressive party.

Mr. Standish sought Mrs. Browne. The landlady was lachrymose and muddled. To his inquiries concerning the queer notion Meg had concerning her mother, she gave a rambling account of a mysterious lady who had come to the lodgings accompanied by an older lady. Meg had been born here, and the mother had died in giving her birth. No father had ever come to visit the mother or child.

Mrs. Browne admitted that some money was sent regular through a lawyer— just enough to pay for Meg's clothing and schooling; but who the lawyer was, Mrs. Browne refused to tell.

Mr. Standish left Mrs. Browne drying her eyes, and went up, meditating how to address Meg. There had come to him an indistinct realization of what the thought of a lady-mother had been to the child in her sordid surroundings. After a few moments' deliberation he took out pen, ink, and paper, and wrote in Roman characters:

> "DEAR MEG: I write to ask you to forgive me. You were right, and I was wrong. Your mother was a lady, just as you thought she was. I have heard all about her. Won't you forgive me, and come and see me? I feel lonely without my little friend.
>
> "W. S."

Having folded the letter, he slipped it under the child's door; then he returned to his room and waited, leaving his own door ajar. After awhile he began to sing some of Meg's favorite melodies—"Sally in the Alley" and "Margery

Allen." He thought he heard a furtive step. He turned his head away, so as not to frighten by so much as a glance the shy advance, and began softly to sing Meg's favorite ballad:

"Nellie was a lady—
Last night she died."

He fancied he distinguished the reluctant drawing near of tardy feet. When the song was ended he looked round. Meg was on the threshold. A glance revealed the change those four days had wrought. Her hair was unkempt, her dress untidy, her cheeks pale; but it was not so much those signs of neglect, the pallor of her cheeks, the drawn lines about her mouth that startled him, as a certain expression of childish recklessness. It was the Meg he had seen wrangling with boys in the street, flying past him lawless and fierce. In her hand she held his letter, and she kept her eyes fixed upon him with a bold stare.

"Is it true what you have written here, or is it a pack of stories?" she asked abruptly.

"It is all true, Meg," said Mr. Standish gently. "She was a lady."

"A real lady, like those that drive about in the carriages?" asked the child with stern cross-examination.

"She was a real lady, Meg; just as you have always pictured her—with soft hands that had never done rough work, and a gentle voice. All about her was beautiful," replied Mr. Standish in slow and convinced tones.

At this assurance Meg gave a little sigh; the tension about her lips relaxed; the fierce brilliancy of her interrogative glance was subdued.

"How do you know?" she asked more softly.

"Mrs. Browne told me. I will take you to her, and she will tell it to you."

"I don't want her to tell me, you tell me," said Meg quickly.

Mr. Standish hesitated; under the child's innocent gaze he found it difficult to speak. He told her in simple words some of the story Mrs. Browne had related. It was a mercy Meg evinced no curiosity concerning her father. Mr. Standish dwelt upon the beauty, the youth, the suffering of the mother; he spoke of the love she had lavished in anticipation upon the babe she was never to see.

As he spoke, the thought of that early and lonely death thrust itself before him with a new and piteous force. The thought of the forsaken child moved him, and his voice faltered.

Meg was by his side in a moment; her hand touched his. "You asked me in your letter to forgive you," she whispered. "I forgive you."

He took the little hand. "You must forget also, Meg, that I said your mother had left you poor and uncared for."

"But she did. She left me poor, and with strangers; that's what you said," replied Meg, with a return of the old fierceness, quoting his words.

"She died," he answered with emphasis, bending forward. "Listen, Meg," he continued, as the child remained apparently unsoftened, "will you believe me, even if you do not understand me—will you believe me?"

For a moment Meg remained dogged and silent, then, as she met his troubled glance, the doubt passed from hers, the confiding light came back.

"I believe you; I believe you very much," she said.

"Then, when you think of her, Meg, think that some one had done her great injury—had made her suffer, more than you can know. That is why she came here and died. She left you poor because everything had been taken from her."

He paused a moment. Meg was pale, and seemed a little dazed; but the excitement had left her manner.

"Everything," he repeated with emphasis.

The child's bosom heaved.

"Now that she is dead," resumed the young man, "I believe that dear mother watches over her little daughter."

"You believe it," said Meg slowly.

"I believe it," said Mr. Standish. "But, come; where is that picture? Let me look at it again."

Meg was off and back again in a moment. The print was torn and besmeared, as if it had gone through rough usage since he had seen it last.

"Halloo! it is falling to bits. It was not so crumpled and torn the other day," he remarked.

"No," Meg confessed; "I hated it the other night, when you said mother was hard-working, like a charwoman. I wanted to tear it up—I did; but I could not." She stopped; for the first time there came a choking in her throat, and a sob, quickly repressed.

Mr. Standish pretended absorption in his occupation, spread out the tattered print, and announced his intention of bestowing to the painting a new lease of life by pasting it upon a pasteboard back. He gathered the necessary implements for the task. Meg, usually so active, watched in silence; but he knew, by the trembling of the little hand resting on the table, by the stiff uprightness of the small figure beside him, the fierce battle the child was waging with herself to suppress all show of emotion.

He took no apparent heed of her, but proceeded with the task of renovation. Perhaps he had intended still to lead the child's mind to a truer conception of a lady than she could get from worship of this simpering fetish, with a mouth like a cherry, and curled eyelashes; but as he handled the old fashion-plate, the pathos of its smeared and battered condition touched him with a sense of sacredness, and he found himself declaring that her mother might have been like that picture. There was no doubt about it; it represented a lovely creature, and her mother was a lovely lady.

When the task was completed he was rewarded by the sight of Meg's radiant countenance. In perfect peace she carried off the restored picture.

CHAPTER II.

TWO YEARS LATER.

Two years had elapsed, and to superficial observers Meg might have appeared to have changed only by some inches added to her length of limb. She still haunted the corner overlooking the stairs on the topmost lobby, but it was not to watch the come and go of the shabby social eddies breaking down below. She read much to herself. Her choice of literature was a queer *mélange* of odds and ends. She was up to all the fires, the accidents, the pageants of a world into which she had never set foot. She knew to what corner of a London daily paper and provincial weekly she was to look to find descriptions of these sensational incidents, and the style in which they were recorded stirred in her an admiration worthy of being lavished on Homeric epics. She knew also a number of ballads by heart that she would recite with an amount of native dramatic vividness.

If the shifting scenes going on downstairs no longer attracted her as in the past, she was intent and absorbed in watching one life. The friendship between her and Mr. Standish had become a tie that drew out peculiarities of the child's nature. There had been quarrels, coolnesses, reconciliations, but Meg's usual attitude toward the journalist was one of mingled proprietorship and watchfulness. It was a mixture of motherly solicitude and dog-like faithfulness. She cross-questioned, admonished, and kept vigilant guard over his interests.

Once, having discovered that Mrs. Browne had cheated him of sixpence in the weekly bill, she drew the landlady's notice to the overcharge; but Mrs. Browne refused to acknowledge or set it right, and Meg cried herself to sleep. Loyalty to the landlady was discarded, and with brimming eyes and quivering lips she told Mr. Standish next day of that fraudulent sixpence. To her dismay he laughed, and vowed that Mrs. Browne's name ought to be handed down to posterity as an honest landlady if sixpence covered the amount of a week's cheating. Meg would not be comforted; to her the landlady seemed remorseless.

A mother could not have detected with quicker apprehension a shade of weariness or pallor on the young man's face. Her invariable question on such an occasion would be, "What have you had for dinner?" Sometimes he tried to deceive her. He would roll out a dazzling *menu*—turtle soup, turbot, plum-pudding.

She would stop him at once with pathetic and angry remonstrance. "It is not true; you know it is not true. Why do you say it?"

Her earnestness always moved him; he was ashamed of deceiving her.

Their last quarrel had been caused by Mr. Standish's confession that he had dined off fish.

"Fish!" cried Meg with scorn, tossing her head. "Can you work after a bit of fish? What fish—turbot, salmon, fried soles?" The ladies who occupied the drawing-room floor gave occasional dinner-parties, where such delicacies figured.

As Mr. Standish kept shaking his head, the smile in his eyes growing more amused and tender, a terrible idea dawned upon Meg. She grew pale.

"Herring!" she faltered.

"Herrings," he repeated in a voice of rich appreciation. "Two herrings, fat as lord mayors!"

Meg walked about the room, her eyes bright with angry misery, her lips trembling. "It's downright wicked! You want to kill yourself, that's what you want to do." She flicked a tear away. "A workman in the street down there has a better dinner than that."

"Now, Meg, be reasonable," the young man pleaded in a voice of protest. "Don't you see," he went on, striking his left palm with two fingers of the right hand, "there is a day called 'pay-day' that rules my bill of fare, as I explained to you the other day the moon rules the tides. On pay-day and its immediate followers I live in abundance. Then come days of lesser luxuries, then abstinence. I have reached this period. Soon plenty will reign again."

"It is a foolish way of managing money," said Meg, abrupt in her trouble, and only half-comforted.

"Can you tell me, Meg, how to manage money without reference to pay-day?" he asked.

"Will you do as I tell you?" she said, stopping short in her restless peregrinations.

He nodded.

"Take your money, all your money, and divide it into little parcels, as many parcels as there are days it must last, and every day spend just what is inside one of the little parcels, and not a bit more," said Meg with elucidating gestures.

Mr. Standish vowed she spoke like a chancellor of the exchequer; that the more he heard her the more he was determined on coming into the colossal fortune he was to enjoy some day, to appoint her his almoner, housekeeper, the dispenser of his bounties, the orderer of his dinners. This project to be his housekeeper was one dear to Meg's heart, the pacifier of her wrath. By what means Mr. Standish was to come into possession of this fabulous wealth remained vague. Sometimes he would announce his intention of getting it by marrying an heiress, a project always chillingly received by Meg. Sometimes she would suggest spitefully that the heiress would not marry him; but Mr. Standish overrode all objections, and would depict days of indolent delight for himself and his bride, while Meg managed the household. When the daydream reached this point it generally abruptly terminated by Meg plunging out of the room, and banging the door after her with an emphatic "Shan't!"

On the evening of the fish dinner Mr. Standish left the heiress out of the question, and Meg was softened.

The next day the young man supped at home. His tray, as usual on these occasions, was brought in by Meg. A burly German sausage and a pot of Scotch marmalade graced the board. Meg's answers were evasive concerning the source from which these dainties came. It struck Mr. Standish that Meg had bought them with the store of half-pence he had taught her to put away in a moneybox he had himself presented to her, with a view to inculcating economical instincts. Her fierce refusal to answer convinced him that he had guessed right.

The refusal to touch these dainties died on his lips. He could not hurt the child. He ate the supper she had provided with loud laudations of its excellence. Before it was finished an arrangement had been entered into between them. On pay-day Meg would henceforth receive a sum to be kept for him against the days of privation. The contract had been fulfilled. Meg had proved a stern treasurer, resisting the young man's entreaties to dole out portions of the money before the appointed time.

If the child had gained much by intercourse with an educated mind, if her English had grown by it more refined and correct, her mind stored with more definite and varied knowledge; if, above all, there had come to her by this affection a precocious womanliness, taming and sweetening her lonely life, Mr. Standish had gained as much by the tie between them. A sort of wonder, half-amused, half-tender, sometimes awoke in his heart at the thought of the child's devotion. His occupation led him to see rough sides of life, and as he became familiar with degradation, the goodness, the innocence of the child was ever before him. He felt it was touching to be loved by a child of ten. Her advanced wisdom struck him. If it stirred his sense of humor and inclined him to laugh, still it made him thoughtful.

During those two years he had enlarged his connections. He was earning more money. Individuals, somewhat of unkempt appearance, whom Meg disapproved of thoroughly, often made their way up the stairs to the young man's rooms. The peals of laughter, the loud talk emerging from the sanctum, confirmed Meg in judging these visitors foolish company for her hero. The child grew hot with angry apprehension when the bell rang shortly after their coming, and Jessie would answer it with tumblers of whisky and lemons. On letting out these friends Meg thought that Mr. Standish usually looked excited, his eyes brighter, his manner more expansive. The child grew restless, alert, suspicious. She did not disguise her feelings to Mr. Standish. Why did these rough men come drinking his whisky? She would break into fierce denunciations against drink.

"Madam"—Mrs. Browne—"always said she was poor. Why was she poor? Because she was always a-sipping and drinking. He'd keep being poor too."

Often Meg's tones, staccato with prophetic denunciation, would falter at the picture she evoked.

Mr. Standish listened sometimes with an amused and indulgent good humor that exasperated Meg; sometimes an uneasy qualm was perceptible in his voice as he admitted that Meg was wise; sometimes he assumed a superior tone of disapproval that silenced her for the time, but left her more than ever under the shadow of a vague and sorrowful apprehension.

One Sunday afternoon Mr. Standish emerged from his room ready to sally forth. Meg appeared out of her shadowy corner.

"Going out?" she asked shortly.

He nodded, smiling down with benign amusement. He seemed enveloped in a holiday brightness.

"Going with those horrid men?" she resumed, throwing her words out with sorrowful brevity.

He nodded, and drew out his watch. He was apparently in a mood to be entertained.

"Come, Meg, there are five minutes for a sermon. I will listen to it respectfully, as if it were the Archbishop of Canterbury preaching."

But Meg was too much absorbed to mind a joke. She followed him into his sitting-room, and began restlessly walking about.

Mr. Standish sat down, and as he stroked his hat with his sleeve he watched the little figure's perambulations. Meg wore her Sunday gown, a rusty black velveteen, foldless and clinging, buttoned from throat to hem. She had outgrown its scanty proportions. Her feet, incased in black felt slippers, looked large under the trim ankles.

"Well, Meg, I am waiting," said Mr. Standish.

"Don't go," said the child, stopping short and facing him abruptly. The quaint austerity of the skimpy garment brought out the lines of the childish figure as she stood erect and animated before him.

"Why not, Meg?"

"Because they're bad; because I hate them; because they'll bring you to misery," said the child, with an upward flash of one little brown well-formed hand, and with a piteous emphasis on the last word.

"Nonsense, Meg!" said Mr. Standish, impatient because more impressed than he cared to be. "You keep comparing my friends with Mrs. Browne—I don't mean any disrespect—an uneducated tippling old woman. My friends, my dear Meg, are gentlemen, educated men, who, I admit, are fond of a joke, fond of a glass or two glasses of grog, but who respect themselves."

"Education has nothing to do with it," snapped Meg, with concise energy. "There was a man downstairs, he was educated. I think he was the devil. He'd leave his wife and little child for days, and come back drunk." Meg gave a fierce little shudder. "There'd be scenes. One day he went and never came back—never, and the wife and baby boy went off one snowy day to the workhouse."

"Poor child, you should not see those things!" said Mr. Standish with a troubled look.

"Why not? You would not let these men up there take your money if you saw them."

There was a grotesque sweetness in Meg's appearance as she stood there in her skimpy dress, her short dusky hair falling in masses about her neck and over her forehead. There came to the young journalist a remembrance of those wingless angels that the pre-Raphaelite masters painted, gracious, grave, workaday beings, with unearthly wise faces. But it was not as a picture that he contemplated Meg; the thought of the goodness, the purity, the holiness of the child, who knew so much and understood so little of life, overcame him. Her innocence almost frightened him. He felt the sacredness of a vow taken to her; it would be more binding than one taken before a court of justice.

"What is it that you want me to promise, Meg?" he asked.

"Not to let them take your money from you, not to let them give you drink," she replied with her accustomed unhesitancy, but her voice faltering with harbored longing.

"Not drink at all?" he asked.

"I wish not at all; I wish not at all," she replied with unconscious repetition.

"Look here, Meg; I'll promise you this—I'll not waste my money, and I'll not tipple like Mrs. Browne downstairs. Will that satisfy you?"

"You promise!" said Meg vehemently, with another upward flash of the well-formed little brown hand, and holding him with her eyes.

"I promise," said Mr. Standish gravely, disguising an inclination to laugh.

The young man was busy in the intervals of journalistic work composing a political squib. He had not so much time to devote to Meg as in the less-employed days, but he allowed her to sit near him when he wrote, reading the story-books and ballads he gave her. In his leisure, as he smoked his pipe, he watched with half-closed eyes the quaint little figure, and drew the child out to talk. He explained the difficult passages in the books she read, and gave her lessons in recitation. Better than anything to Meg, he sometimes imparted to her the last *bon mot* he had put into the mouth of "Sultan Will" to his suffering subjects—a confidence that invariably produced abnormal gravity in Meg.

The child had no reason to think the young man was not fulfilling the promise he had given. His alert carriage and concentrated expression contradicted any suspicion of faltering. Yet she was restless; his friends came often to see him.

"Why did they come, disturbing him at his work?" she asked spitefully.

Mr. Standish called her a hard little taskmaster, and received his friends cordially. A formless fear was at the child's heart. She haunted the threshold of his door when they were in his room; she lay awake of nights when she knew that he had gone out with them. She magnified to herself the number of times that he had gone out earlier and come home later than he used. If she dropped asleep her slumbers were broken until she heard the sound of his footsteps on the stairs.

One evening Mr. Standish went off in company with two journalistic comrades to a public dinner, given to members of the press by the directors of a new railway company. Meg would not retract the unfavorable verdict she pronounced upon his appearance in the new dress suit he had ordered specially for the occasion. She was not to be mollified by the promise of an orange from the directors' table. "She did not want an orange; she did not see what a dinner had to do with a railway," she averred.

That night she could not sleep. The formless fear at her heart lay heavy upon it; it seemed to her that the fulfillment of that nameless dread was approaching. As the hour came and passed Mr. Standish had fixed for his return, visions began to group about her bed and pass before her wide-open eyes. All the sorrowful stories of accidents Mr. Standish had related to her enacted themselves before her, in which he appeared the central figure. The night plodded slowly on; the clock in the hall struck the hours at intervals. When the clock struck three Meg got up and paced about the room, a wan little ghost.

When another hour struck the four peals sounded like a hammer-stroke on a coffin. Meg began to dress. She did not know why she did so, or what she would do after, but a vague sense of being needed impelled her. She fumbled her way to the staircase and sat on the topmost step.

She waited in the darkness and silence. A faint whiteness began to steal through the sides of the blinds drawn over the window on the lobby. The banisters, the flight of stairs, showed shadowily, gradually growing more distinct.

Suddenly she sprang to her feet. There was the scrape of a key in the latch. A step sounded in the hall, made its way up the stairs. It was Mr. Standish. When he reached the topmost flight of steps he perceived the little gray figure standing waiting in the gray dawn, erect, immobile. He steadied himself against the banisters and began to laugh. He looked pale, his eyes dark; his hat was thrown back, his hair disordered.

"Why, Meg, you little detective, are you there? Such a jolly night! splendid dinner! No humbug this time, Meg—real turtle, tuns of champagne!" He came up a few steps. "Tuns of champagne, Meg! Speeches, Meg! Such nonsense! Everybody complimented everybody else. I did not forget you, Meg. Look here, I stole an orange and sweetmeats!" He began fumbling in his pockets.

"You've broken your promise," said the child in a low and trembling voice.

"Not a bit of it, Meg. Now you think I am tipsy," he replied, speaking huskily. "Not a bit of it. You'll see if I can't walk straight as a lamp post to that door."

As he went up he staggered—she had not seen him stumble before—caught himself by the balustrade, then plunged forward with uneven steps.

Instinctively Meg put out her hand, but he did not see it. Catching at the wall he fell into a fit of laughing; then making his way to his room he let the door slam behind him.

Meg was petrified. All that she had dreaded seemed to have happened. She sat down, her throat burning, her body cold, as if a shroud enfolded her. She remained huddled and moveless until signs of life began to be heard in the house. Then she got up and crept into her attic.

CHAPTER III.

MEG TO THE RESCUE.

Mr. Standish saw no more of Meg for some days. He made no attempt at reconciliation. It amused him to think how Meg magnified his offense. It seemed comical that the child should set him down as a drunkard. He laughed out loud over it as he drank his single glass of lager beer at dinner. In his workaday life he avoided taking his glass of grog. He never indulged in it, for economical reasons. With his brothers of the press he took a convivial glass, but as for squandering money, he had none to spend.

After a few days, as Meg remained sternly invisible, he began to miss her, as a man might miss a favorite dog. To his inquiries concerning the child, Mrs. Browne or Jessie replied, she was "that" cross there was no biding her.

If he caught a glimpse of Meg she would vanish at his approach, and no call or song could entice her from her retreat. Then Mr. Standish made up his mind the child was absurdly unjust, and that in time she would come round; still he was more sorry than he allowed himself to acknowledge at her desertion. His work had grown upon him, an old debt harassed him, and he had lately received a sufficiently unpleasant surprise to occupy his mind.

Meanwhile, the passionate little figure, hidden in the shadow of the half-open door, watched his coming and going with keener vigilance. From her hiding-place the child scanned his countenance as he came and went; and at night fell into broken slumbers, until the sound of his returning footsteps brought peace to her unquiet heart. If Meg had known how to pray, or had realized that she could effectively and without indecorum pray out of church, she would have climbed in spirit to the throne of the Most High, and with insistent appeal have interceded for the friend she confusedly felt was passing through some dread peril. But Meg's conception of the world beyond the grave was as of a great darkness, against which outlined itself a simpering countenance wreathed with roses, which was her mother's face. To that dear vision Meg was eloquent concerning her grief—brokenly, and with impatient and angry misery, murmured to it of Mr. Standish's breach of faith, of the certain ruin that was waiting him, and of her own wretchedness.

Mr. Standish's ways completely puzzled her, and the mystery added to that desperate sense of estrangement between them. Some time before their quarrel she had watched one day a shabby-genteel-looking man knock at the journalist's door, and, on its being opened, hand to Mr. Standish a paper which he received and glanced over, the child noticed, with an expression of surprised consternation. He did not invite the visitor in. Meg could not distinguish the purport of the talk that ensued between them, but heard Mr.

Standish's last words, in the anxiously confident tones of which, she detected a ghost of displeasure: "There has been some delay, but give me time to write again to him and I am sure it will be all right."

On her inquiries concerning this mysterious visitor, with a face she described as a red plum-pudding, Mr. Standish had given evasive answers. From that day she noted, however, that he changed his hours of going out; he appeared anxious; he locked his door after him. Sometimes, as a pledge of confidence, he had left his key with her, and he had told her not to let anyone in during his absence.

A week after their falling out, Meg, in looking over the superscription of Mr. Standish's letter in the hall, recognized the delicate and familiar handwriting of one of the young man's friends—who was also her favorite antipathy. She had at one time often brought epistles in this handwriting that she suspected were begging petitions. This letter bore a foreign stamp.

That afternoon Mr. Standish's voice, for the first time since his quarrel, was uplifted in song. As he went out he paused, and softly called "Meg." But Meg, in the shadow, straightened herself; an aggressive light brightened her eyes; she hesitated. Had he called again she might have come, but with a half-vexed laugh and a shrug he ran downstairs.

For the first time, also, he had left the key in his door. The child stole toward the room, opened the door, and looked in. Her heart smote her with remorse and pity as she beheld the disorder, the uncared-for confusion that reigned within—slippers pitched at different corners of the room; the tobacco-pouch half emptying its contents in a manuscript, the dust lying heavy on papers and books, the boot-jack inside the silver inkstand that had belonged to his father.

In a moment Meg was at her old task of setting the room in order. Flitting hither and thither, she zealously dusted, swept, put the books back into their accustomed places. She knew exactly where every volume was to stand. As she scrubbed and worked, the hard knot at her little heart loosened. She had proceeded some way at her task when she came upon a paper. She recognized the nature of the paper at a glance; she had seen such a missive in Mrs. Browne's possession before. It was a summons to appear before the county court. She read the words on the paper. The summons was taken out by one Abraham Samuels, who held a bill overdue for £25. The court was to sit on Wednesday, November 16th. To-day was the 26th—ten days later.

Meg stood stock-still with the paper in her hand. This was the paper the strange man had brought. She thought of Mr. Standish's brightened mood; what did it mean? Had he paid the debt? A tear dropped on the summons as she dwelt upon that past anxiety. How could she atone for having kept away so sternly? The only way that presented itself to her mind for displaying the energy of her repentance was by rubbing the furniture till it shone in the firelight. She put the last touch to her work by filling the two vases with late autumn foliage and yellow chrysanthemums, bought with her remaining pence. It was late that night when the journalist returned, but she noticed that he bounded lightly up the stairs, and she turned happily on her side and fell asleep. Mr. Standish was not up next morning when Meg set off for school.

He was out when she returned. As she was sallying forth on an errand for Mrs. Browne she perceived Jessie in deep confabulation with a smooth-voiced stranger in the hall, who was apparently making himself agreeable to the slavey. At a glance she recognized him to be the stranger with the face like a red plum-pudding, who had handed that summons to Mr. Standish.

In a flash she recollected the key was in the door of the journalist's room. The next moment her bounding young feet had carried her up the stairs, and she had locked the door, and dropped the key into her apron pocket, before the representative of justice came panting up on the scene. Meg's experience of life had included strange branches of education. She had watched the maneuvers of debtors to keep bailiffs at bay, and the strategy of the men in authority to get into possession.

"What do you want?" she inquired, standing before the threshold she was defending.

"I want Mr. Standish—a writing gent. I've got news for him," replied the stranger with an air of business.

"Can't see him," said Meg briefly. "He's out, and the door's locked."

"Now, that's awful unfortunate," replied the visitor, with an air of perplexed consternation. "Those writing gents make their living by getting news, and my news is so important that he ought to know it."

"What news is it? I'll tell him when he comes in," said Meg curtly.

"Can't do that, missy. Now, I take it," continued the stranger insinuatingly, "you know where the key of that room is. If you let me in, I'll give you the prettiest, shiniest sixpence you ever saw. Come, now, let me in, and I'll write my news down for the gent. My time's precious-like, you see."

"Who are you? Where do you come from?" asked Meg.

"I come from his newspaper office. I am what these writing gents call a printer's devil, ha, ha, ha!"—and the stranger bubbled over with enjoyment of his own joke.

"You're telling an awful fib," said Meg, red to the roots of her hair. "You are a bailiff. I've seen bailiffs," and she nodded, "and I know their dodges. You want to get into Mr. Standish's room to take his things—that's what you want to do."

"Eh, now, you are clever—as clever as clever can be—the prettiest, cleverest little girl!" rejoined the visitor admiringly.

"Do you think," said Meg, evidently taking no notice of the compliment, "that a man ought to be punished who is always very kind and good, and who works—works so hard—I could not tell you how hard; who eats very little, and who scarcely drinks ever at all—that is, very seldom." Meg dashed away a tear, and went on with energy, advancing with restless steps. "If this good man has friends who are bad, dishonest, lazy drunkards, who take all his money and don't give it back, don't you think it is they who ought to be punished, not the good man?"

"Well, missy, there's a deal in what you say—a deal," said the stranger ponderingly; then, as Meg approached, lost in her pleading, he made a sudden flop forward, and almost clutched her skirt, gasping, "That's a pretty apron, missy—a nice little apron."

But Meg had whisked the apron out of his grasp; and, dancing back, shook the hair out of her eyes. "You wickedest man! trying to get the key out of my pocket! But I'll not let you have it. I'll throw it out of that window into the gutter that runs down there sooner than let you have it." Meg as she spoke opened the window in the lobby, and kept near it.

"Then here I'll sit!" said the bailiff, depositing his burly form on the stair.

"How long will you sit there?" asked Meg.

"That's none of your business. I'll sit till he comes up. I believe he's a scamp. Those hauthors and hartists are. I know lots of 'em. I warrant he's in the tavern spending his money."

"I hate you!" cried Meg with a flash, her bosom heaving, her little red lips drawn tight over her teeth.

There was something pitiably droll in the attitude of the child, standing at a safe distance, clutching her pocket, quivering with helpless wrath, before the impassable persecutor. With a sudden spring she turned and dashed away, pausing to open a little wider the window that let in the draft upon the bailiff.

"You'll get frightful rheumatism waiting there, and I'm glad of it," she cried, as she disappeared.

Mr. Standish, returning half an hour later, saw a small figure promenading up and down before the house under a dripping umbrella. It was Meg. She was by his side in a moment.

"Come this minute," she said, putting her hand into his.

"Why, Meg," he said cheerily, yet surprised at her manner; "so you have forgiven me at last!"

She did not answer; but as he was about to open the hall door with his latchkey, she said laconically, "Not this way," and led him round by the back way.

Meg flitted up the narrow stairs before him, every now and then turning back with forefinger on lips to enjoin silence. Up, up she went, until she reached the attic that was her own room. She signed to him to enter, and then shut the door.

"Why, what is this for, Meg," said Mr. Standish, looking round.

"He's here—the bailiff—waiting on the stairs, but he can't get in. I locked the door and kept the key; here it is." With an expressive twinkle of her eyes she whisked it out of her pocket, and put it into his hand.

Mr. Standish sat down, looked at Meg, scarce understanding. "Bailiff!" he repeated. "Then Gilbert has not paid! I backed his bill because I trusted his sacred promise that he would meet it in time!"

"It was kind, but foolish," said Meg briefly.

"He wrote the other day to say he would make it all right with Samuels, when I told him of the writ. He assured me the money was going by the next post," Mr. Standish went on blankly.

"He's an old cheat," said Meg, with scornful directness of speech.

"What is to be done? I have no money, Meg," said the young man, with a wretched flicker of a smile.

"Pawn your watch and chain—they're real gold; they're big and heavy; they'll raise the money," said Meg, with her usual unhesitancy.

The journalist flushed red. "I can't, Meg!" He drew the watch out of his pocket. It was a large hunting watch, that had been presented to the rector, his father. Inside the lid the names of the donors were inscribed in minute characters. "I can't, Meg," he repeated, looking at it and shaking his head. "A token of affectionate gratitude, a testimonial to his faithful work—I can't place it where there are so many associations that are disgraceful. It would be degradation——"

"Not a bit of it!" said Meg with fearless rapidity, as he rose and walked up and down the attic. "You'll get it back soon. You'll work hard to get it out. If you don't pawn it you'll have to let that man in," nodding in the direction of the staircase. "He'll sit in your room. You'll be able to do no work with him there, smelling of gin, and his red face looking at you. He'll take the silver ink-bottle—and the books. Pawn your watch, and if you work hard you'll get it out soon."

"Wise, practical Meg," said Mr. Standish, scarcely able to repress a smile, moving irresolutely about the little room.

"Give it to me! I'll pawn it for you," rejoined Meg, intent and business-like. "I've been there before. Last time Mrs. Browne put the silver teapot up the spout I went for her. She was tipsy; she could not go. The man knows me. He'll give me the money."

"I have not the heart to do it Meg—I have not the heart," said Mr. Standish, hesitating as the child approached.

"It's better than having the man inside your room, sitting on your green velvet armchair or the chintz sofa, taking the silver ink-bottle and the books, and preventing your working," continued Meg, pressing her advantage; and as Mr. Standish began slowly to unloose the chain, her deft fingers came to the rescue and helped him.

He looked down at the eager, determined child-face. "How good you are to me, Meg; how good!" he said, the words rushing almost unconsciously to his lips.

A quiver of the eyelids only showed the child felt the tones. "Give it to me," she repeated imperatively.

The next moment the watch and chain, wrapped in a clean pocket-handkerchief, were in Meg's grasp, and she had departed. Mr. Standish, stooping under the shelving ceiling on a level with the strip of window, looked out and watched the wet umbrella making its way under the flaring gas and over the muddy street. When it disappeared he turned and looked about him. There was a sincerity, a poverty, a purity about the tiny chamber that affected him with a wholesome shock. Over the little white bed hung the fashion-plate that he had mended, in the pasteboard frame he had manufactured for it. A bit of scarlet ribbon fastened it to a nail, with an elaborate bow. Above it, as a pious Catholic might have crossed about some saint's image branches of blessed palms, so Meg had placed sprigs of lavender, that delicately scented the room. On the peg behind the door hung the little Sunday frock, turned inside out. On a table, under a clean pocket-handkerchief, were placed three books that he had given her—a volume of ballads, "Stories from the History of England," a gaudily illustrated shilling copy of "Cinderella." Also under the pocket-handkerchief was a bundle of paper, tied with scarlet ribbon, that proved to be some of his articles neatly cut out. A black clay pipe of his, which Meg had mended, was put up like a little Indian idol over the table. The little room, so spotlessly clean, and so characteristic in all its details, was distinctly Meg's room, telling of that mystic love for her mother, and of her solitary friendship.

Mr. Standish was not tired of waiting when Meg appeared, her hand clutching the bodice of her dress.

"Here, I've got the money," she said, as carefully pulling out the handkerchief and opening it she displayed a roll covered with paper; "twenty-five pounds—count; and here's the ticket. Don't lose it on any account. Perhaps I'd better keep it for you."

"Twenty-five pounds, Meg!" said Mr. Standish.

"He wanted to give me twenty. I said 'No, twenty-five.' He was smiling when he said twenty. Those men always smile when they want to cheat you," said Meg, with a nod of retrospective observation. "He gave me twenty-five pounds at last, though. Count."

The child cut short the words of thankfulness that rose to Mr. Standish's lips.

"Go," she said imperatively, taking him by the hand and leading him to the door; "pay the man and get him off."

A few minutes later, with great glee, Meg watched the departure of the bailiff; she thought with pleasure as he made his way downstairs that he seemed a little stiff, as if he had got rheumatism. After the hall door had slammed behind the representative of the law she stood hesitating. Soon her diffident feet slowly brought her to Mr. Standish's threshold. She pushed the door softly open. He was sitting by the table, his face covered with his hands. He looked up as she entered.

"He's gone," said Meg, nodding. "Aren't you glad?"

"You have done me a great service, Meg. How can I thank you for it?" said the young man, rising and taking the child's two hands in his.

"Don't thank me—not at all," said Meg with ardor, looking up into his face. "Just promise never to lend your money again—never."

"No—never again!" replied Mr. Standish, shaking his head. He led the child in and sat down, still keeping her hand in his. "How did you guess that man was a bailiff?"

"Oh," said Meg, with the scornful brevity of wide experience in her voice, "I knew him by his sleeky ways. I've watched them at their dodges. They're up to almost anything."

Mr. Standish laughed out loud; but the laugh suddenly fell as he thought of all that knowledge implied. He said gently, after a pause:

"I thought the little friend who used to sit by my fireside had left me. I missed you, Meg."

"You were tipsy that night," the child answered, with a quaver in her voice that did not take from its severity.

"You punished me hard, Meg. Don't you know I had to drink so many healths. There was the queen's health to drink, and I should have been a disloyal subject if I had not drunk that; and there was the lord mayor's health, I should have been a bad citizen if I had not drunk that; then there were the directors' healths, and there were one another's healths." As Meg remained unmollified, he went on, "Meg, I will tell you a secret. I was not so bad as I looked that night—I put it on a little for your benefit."

"That was wicked of you," said Meg with spirit.

"It was," agreed Mr. Standish candidly. "Come, Meg, won't you forgive me if I promise——"

"You promised before," interrupted the child.

A desire to rehabilitate himself in the child's eyes seized Mr. Standish. He felt a touch of awe of that creature regarding him with steady gravity, and he found himself pleading his cause before her as if she were a little chief justice.

"If he got himself into difficulties for his friends, they were often to be pitied; so many in this world were born weak, like spiritual cripples who needed a helping hand."

"No use to them when they get it," said Meg. "They're always in a muddle."

Mr. Standish once more repressed an inclination to laugh at the child's precocious wisdom. He admitted there was truth in what she said. Once, three years ago, just before coming here, he had given all he had to a friend, and it had been of no use.

"Did you lend him much money?" asked Meg.

"Yes; he was in the greatest distress. I loved him, Meg. I would do it again if he came to me. If he was reckless, he was so handsome and so jolly. He came and told me all about his trouble. His father was very stern; he would not see him or help him. My friend wanted three hundred pounds. It was all the money that I had."

"And you gave it?" she said, and stopped.

He nodded.

"Did he never pay you back?" she faltered.

"Never, Meg. It is a sad story. There was some disgrace, and he died."

She did not speak; the fate of the stranger seemed to affect her but little.

"You gave him all your money?" she repeated, and again she paused; then she put out her hand and stroked his head, with a look of tender and ineffable admiration.

CHAPTER IV.

FAREWELL.

There followed a time of perfect happiness for Meg, during which, for a few weeks, she sat by her friend's fireside, watched him at his writing, listened to his reading, ruled over the meals that he took at home, and questioned him concerning those that he took abroad.

On a memorable afternoon they celebrated together, with much pomp, over a banquet of jam puffs and lemonade at a confectioner's shop in the Tottenham Court Road, the redemption from pawn of his father's gold watch and chain. Meg again played the part of *Deus ex machina* in the transaction, and personally paid the ransom of the precious pledge. In honor of the event, Mr. Standish presented her with a copy of Goldsmith's "Animated Nature," with "Meg" printed in gold letters on the cover. The sight of her name thus honored overcame the child. He explained to her, when she appeared inclined to rebuke him for extravagance that the political squib, the jokes which used to have a depressing effect upon her, had brought him the unlooked-for cash.

Shortly after this festivity Mr. Standish's movements once more became erratic. Meg could discover no signs, however, of the symptoms that she feared. He seemed mysteriously elated and full of business, yet he wrote less. He admitted when she questioned him that something was absorbing his time, but his answers were evasive concerning the nature of this new interest. He promised that she would know what it was shortly.

One day Mr. Standish had a long talk with Mrs. Browne over a bottle of sherry, after which he went out and returned late. The landlady was maudlinly effusive over Meg that evening, puzzled the child with her ramblingly affectionate talk, and filled her with vague apprehension. Mr. Standish's answers to Meg's queries were also unsatisfactory.

A few days later a dandified elderly gentleman wearing a frilled shirt visited the journalist. As he was leaving Mr. Standish called Meg in, and introduced her to the visitor as "the child I spoke to you about." The elderly gentleman looked at her peeringly, with his head on one side. He chuckled, patted her cheek, and told her if she were a good girl something wonderful might happen to her. The announcement, far from cheering Meg, deepened the foreboding in her heart.

That evening she softly entered Mr. Standish's room. A confused dread seized her when she saw the floor littered with books and papers lying about in parcels. The journalist was sitting by the fire, abstractedly poking the embers.

Meg touched his elbow. "Are you not going to write to-night?" she asked in a low voice.

"Not to-night, Meg. I am going to talk to you instead."

She remained motionless by his chair, questioning him with her glance only.

Still he did not speak. After a moment or two he said abruptly, "Meg would you like to go to school?"

"I go to school every day. What do you mean?" she asked, looking at him with quick suspicion.

"I mean quite another sort of school—one kept by ladies, and where your schoolfellows would be ladies; where you would make lots of nice friends; and where you will sleep at night instead of——"

"You mean go away from here—quite?" interrupted Meg, growing pale to the lips.

"Yes," he answered.

"What do you want me to go away for?" she demanded, a flash of anger in her eyes.

"Because I do not like to leave you with no one but Mrs. Browne to look after you; and I am going away."

"When?" she asked tremulously.

"To-morrow."

She gave an exclamation that sounded like a cry.

He drew her to him.

"Listen, Meg. It will make me very unhappy if I think you are fretting when I am gone. I want my little friend to be brave; she must not fret."

"Where are you going?" she faltered, mastering her emotion.

"I am going to travel and write accounts of what I see, for a newspaper that will pay me very well. It is a great lift for me, Meg, and I want you to have your lift also."

She did not speak, but kept her eyes fixed upon his face. He then gently and guardedly told her that he had got from Mrs. Browne the name of the family solicitor who paid for her keep. He had gone to see him to speak of Meg.

The elderly gentleman with the frilled shirt, who had patted her on the head, was the solicitor in question. His name was Mr. Fullbloom. The young man did not tell the child that he had found out how shamefully misapplied by the landlady was the allowance she received, nor did he tell her that he had made in writing a vivid statement of her forlorn and neglected condition in the boarding-house.

He laid as light stress as he could on the refusal of the solicitor to give up the name of the child's mysterious patron.

"Some one takes a great interest in you, Meg," he said in conclusion; "and Mr. Fullbloom came to assure me from that person that you would now be placed in a first-rate school, where you will have plenty of comrades of your own age, teachers who will care for you; and you will grow up to be a little lady, like your mother in the picture."

Meg listened cold and silent to the end.

"Won't you be glad to go to school to be educated?"

"No," she answered, stiffening herself and jerking out her words, relapsing in her excitement into her old pronunciation. "I will hate going. I don't want to be edicated. What do I want to be edicated for? And if you cared for me you would not wish me to go away, you would not."

Tears stood in her eyes, but anger kept them from falling.

"Do you wish to remain here when I am gone Meg?" he asked.

"No," she replied faintly, as if her heart failed her at the suggestion. "Why can't I go where you go? Who'll light your fire for you, who'll look after you? You want somebody to look after you."

"I know it, Meg, and no one would look after me as you would."

"I'd not want much to eat or drink," Meg went on, alive to the economical side of the question; "and once you said you felt lonely without me."

"So I will, Meg," he answered, drawing her nearer and keeping his arm about her. "And it is just because I care for you that I want you to go to school, that I want you to learn all that can be taught you. I want your little hands to grow soft, that now are hard with housework for me."

The child's face worked, but she controlled the rising sob.

"Listen, Meg. It may be in five years, it may be in six years, it may be when you are a tall, accomplished young girl of eighteen, I shall come to the school where you are, and—" He paused.

"Take me home to be your housekeeper?" said Meg.

A laugh drifted to his face.

"Better than that. We will be friends, close friends, such friends as never were, if you go to this school," he said.

"You promise?" said the child, holding him with her eyes.

He nodded. "I promise, Meg."

"Then I will go to that school," she said submissively, putting her hand into his.

Until eight o'clock, when she usually said good-night, Meg helped Mr. Standish to pack up. She asked to be allowed to remain up a little longer, but he refused the petition.

"It is not good-by, Meg; it is good-night only," he said cheerily, stroking her head; then stooping, he kissed the child's forehead. "God bless you, little Meg!"

Meg did not go to bed. She made no pretense to undress. She lay on the floor of her attic all night, letting the solitude of the coming years pass in anticipation over her heart. In the gray of the morning some furtive sounds reached her ears, and she sprang up listening. A few moments after, Mr. Standish, portmanteau in hand, emerged from his room. A gray little figure stood waiting for him in the dim dawn, as it had waited for him once before. It was Meg, pressing something to her heart.

"My child, I had hoped, I had planned to avoid this for you," he said. "I hoped you would be asleep."

MEG PRESENTS THE OLD FASHION-PLATE TO HER FRIEND.—Page 61.

The child's lips moved, but she did not speak. Abruptly stretching out the hand that she had held pressed against her bosom she put something into his. It was the fashion-plate that had been to her as her mother's portrait.

"Is that for me, Meg?" he asked.

She nodded.

"I'll keep it safe. I'll give it back to you, Meg, when we meet again," he replied, tenderly folding the battered print and laying it inside his pocket-book.

The child kept a stern silence.

"We'll meet again, Meg; I promise you that. Poor little Meg!" he said feelingly. "It is hard for you; but I will write to you—I will write. No one will ever care for me as you have cared."

He kissed her, and as still she preserved the stern silence of repressed grief he turned quickly away. As he ran down he looked back and saw the child watching him, with her face thrust through the banisters.

He waved his hand to her and smiled. The next moment the hall door clapped below, and from above there came the sound of sobbing in the darkness.

CHAPTER V.

A MYSTERIOUS VISIT.

A few days after, in the early afternoon, as Meg was sitting on the floor in her attic with the bundle of articles given her by Mr. Standish spread out on her lap, the books he had given her on the floor around her, the door opened and Mrs. Browne entered.

Meg had been silent and repellent since her friend's departure. She had lived alone, communing with her grief.

The landlady sat down on the child's bed and began rocking herself backward and forward, uttering faint moans.

Meg looked at her gravely and apparently unmoved.

"What are you crying for?" she asked at last, when Mrs. Browne's moans became too emphatic to be passed over in silence.

"I am going to lose you, Meg—after all these years—There's a gentleman downstairs—waiting to take you away. Oh! oh! oh!" moaned Mrs. Browne.

"A gentleman—what gentleman?" asked Meg with trembling eagerness, a light springing to her eyes, for her thoughts had flown to her only friend.

"A kind gentleman—Mr. Fullbloom—You must remember, Meg, as I always said—Mr. Fullbloom—pays for you regular—regular as quarter-day comes, he pays. Remember, as I always said it—And now he's come to take you away from me—who loves you as a mother."

"Is he coming to take me away to that school?" asked Meg, sitting up straight, speaking in curt and business-like tones.

"Yes, you're to go to a school—a grander school—a ladies' school—and you'll forget me, who loved you like a mother."

Meg did not answer. She began to prepare rapidly for her departure. She was going to the school; and this was the first step toward rejoining Mr. Standish in the future.

She paid no heed to Mrs. Browne's feeble grieving over the shabbiness of her wardrobe, her unmended boots, and to the landlady's repeated injunctions to "speak up for me who has been good to you as a mother to the gentleman." Every week, Mrs. Browne protested, she had meant to buy Meg a pretty dress and hat.

"What do I want with a fine dress at school for? I am going to learn—that's what I am going to do. I am going to be a lady," said Meg severely, locking the writing-case, a present from Mr. Standish, in which she had deposited her bundle of articles, and wrapping her books in brown paper.

"The gentleman says you're to take nothing with you except just what will go in a little bag," said Mrs. Browne; "and I've brought you my best hand-bag."

"I'll not go away without these things," said Meg ardently. "I'll not go to school or nowhere without them."

Mrs. Browne shook her head; but Meg was not to be moved.

A few minutes' later, attired in her Sunday garments, her feet shod in worn boots, Meg, carrying her parcel, went downstairs, followed by Mrs. Browne. In the best parlor stood the gentleman she had once seen in Mr. Standish's room, and to whom she had been introduced as the "little girl I spoke to you of."

He still wore a frilled shirt and tapped a silver snuffbox, and he looked at Meg with his head very much on one side.

"Ready to go—ready to go!" he said in a quick chirping voice. "Not crying, eh? not crying?"

Meg disengaged her hand to take the one proffered to her.

"Can't take that parcel," said Mr. Fullbloom, shaking his head. "Can't take it."

"Then I won't go away—I won't go to the school without it," said Meg with fierce decision.

"Tut, tut, tut!" said the lawyer. "What's inside it? Lollipops, eh? lollipops?"

"No," said Meg, pale with eagerness; "it's books and things—keepsakes. I'll never part with them—never!"

"Oh, hoity-toity!" said Mr. Fullbloom, then impressed with the child's resolute look. "Well, well," he added, jerking his head to the other side, "perhaps we'll find a place for it in the carriage."

Then once more Mrs. Browne lifted up her voice, and weeping embraced Meg, who submitted to her caress with a certain stiff-backed irresponsiveness. It is probable that if Meg had been called under other circumstances to leave the gloomy old boarding-house and the boozy landlady, about whom clustered all the associations of her childhood, she would have felt the pang of the uprooting; but an absorbing affection now filled her little heart, and with it had come new hopes and ambition.

A brougham was waiting at the door. Into it she stepped, and after her, Mr. Fullbloom. The next moment she was driving swiftly and silently along. It was all very strange; yet Meg did not feel surprised. Grief had lifted her unconsciously to a higher level of expectation; all unknowingly her attitude toward life was changed.

She was vaguely aware that she was the object of her companion's amused and attentive observation. For all his waggish ways and darting movements Mr. Fullbloom had a shrewd and observant mind. He was a lawyer, accustomed to note with discriminating eye external signs that gave him the clew to the personality of those with whom he came in contact. It had grown to be a second nature with him to take note of appearances. This little maid's imperturbable demeanor before the tears of Mrs. Browne, her quick, fearless trust in him, her determined attitude toward the bundle covered with brown paper, piqued his curiosity, and moved a deeper interest in her than that which he usually accorded to children. The clear-cut little profile, he acknowledged, had a character of its own. Meg's attitude, as she sat upright and somewhat stiffly, partook of the same individuality. Mr. Fullbloom noted every detail of the child's dress—the well-worn turban hat crowning the brown crop of hair, the shabby velveteen dress, the weather-beaten jacket with its border of mangy fur, the old boots, the darned worsted gloves covering the hands that clasped the parcel.

"I think I know a little girl who is not very sorry to leave the old house—not sorry," he said at last, stooping forward and cocking his head with that bird-like swiftness.

"I want to go to that school. Are we going there now?" inquired Meg.

"Perhaps we are—perhaps we are not—perhaps we are going to a fairy palace," replied Mr. Fullbloom with a suggestive sidelong glance.

Meg looked at him smilelessly.

"There are no fairies," she said curtly. "Am I going to that school?"

"Before I tell I want to know who gave you those keepsakes—who was it? The clever young gentleman who took such an interest in little Miss Meg, and who had set his heart so much upon her going to school—was it?" said Mr. Fullbloom facetiously, laying his hand upon the bundle.

"Mr. Standish," answered Meg softly; and the lawyer was astonished at the emotion perceptible on the child's face. It seemed to quiver like the chords of a harp upon which a hand is laid.

The silence was broken, and the lawyer began to question. Meg was guarded and reticent in her monosyllabic replies; but by a few leading questions the lawyer got from her what he wished to know.

He became satisfied that the picture Mr. Standish had drawn of her isolation, neglect, and half-servile position in the boarding-house was unexaggerated. His veiled cross-examination was scarcely concluded before the brougham drew up before a large house overlooking a square, in which tall trees cast their shade athwart the smoothly shaven turf.

"Was this grand house the lady's school?" thought Meg.

A solemn man in black opened the door; an imposing being in a gold-buttoned coat, plush breeches, and silk stockings came forward, and Meg by a dexterous move just rescued her parcel from his officious clutches.

Mr. Fullbloom led her into a side room, saying as he left her that he would be back immediately. The firelight glowed upon frames and mirrors, delicate porcelains, and blue satin hangings. For a few moments the little Cinderella figure remained standing immobile amid these surroundings, lost in wonder, then the lawyer returned, and taking her by the hand conducted her upstairs.

Who was she going to see now? Was she about to be brought before the master or mistress of this fairy palace?

Meg was aware of passing through a room larger and more splendid than the one she had just left. Then Mr. Fullbloom pushed open a door and ushered her into another room furnished with bookcases filled with books, a long table, and dark leather chairs.

An old gentleman was sitting there. His chair was against the window, so that his face was in shadow, but his white hair shone. He was leaning back; there was something rigid in his attitude; his long white hands grasped the arms of the chair.

"Here is the little girl," said Mr. Fullbloom.

The white-haired gentleman made no sign of greeting, and did not speak for a moment; but a close observer might have noticed, even in that half-light, a slight twitch of the old hand.

"You are the little girl who spent all your life in Mrs. Browne's boarding-house?" he said at last, abruptly.

"Yes, sir," said Meg with a quiver in her voice.

In her heart she thought the elderly gentleman was not to be compared in appearance with the glittering footman; but his chill stare seemed to freeze her.

"You remember no other place? You have never been to another?" he asked.

"I remember other places, but I have never lived in another place," said Meg with her usual accuracy.

"What is your name?"

"Meg."

"Meg what?"

"Browne," said Meg.

"No, that is not your name. Beecham is your name. Don't forget—Beecham."

"Beecham?" repeated Meg, amazed.

"Take off your hat!" said her interlocutor.

Meg lifted her left hand to obey, but the elastic caught in her hair, and she put her precious parcel down to free her right hand.

"You were to take nothing out of that house," said the old gentleman sternly.

"I won't give them up—I won't!" cried Meg with kindling countenance, and with hands outstretched to protect her parcel.

"You won't!" repeated the old gentleman with frozen severity. Mr. Fullbloom bent over his chair. There was a whispered colloquy. Then the old gentleman said in a voice that might have been that of an audible icicle: "You may keep those things if you do not ask for anything else."

"I do not want anything else," said Meg with energy.

"Turn to the light."

Meg, all rebellion smoothed from her countenance, turned, obedient as a light-haunting flower, toward the gleam of sunshine filtering through the heavy curtains. The light fell caressingly on the spirited little face in its renewed quietude.

"That will do," said the old gentleman; and he fell into a brooding silence.

"This little girl wants to grow up a learned little lady—a learned little lady," put in Mr. Fullbloom cheerily after a pause.

"Yes, that is what I want to be," answered Meg with an eager nod.

"If you are sent to school," resumed the stranger sternly, bending on the child a glance that seemed to her to be one of aversion, "you must promise never to speak of that time spent in the boarding-house. You are to forget everything that happened there, and everybody you met there."

"I'll not forget every one. There is one person I will never forget—never," replied Meg with energy.

"Mr. Standish, the young man who was her friend. Can't ask her to forget him yet—can't do that," put in Mr. Fullbloom in a tone of jaunty conciliation, shaking his head. "I feel sure Meg will not speak about him."

"I don't want to talk about him," said Meg, her voice instinct with the sacredness of her affection.

"Do you know how to read?" asked the old gentleman.

"Yes," replied Meg briefly.

Her mysterious questioner opened a volume, turned rapidly over the pages until he came to one where a chapter ended. He passed his forefinger over the page with a heaviness that widened the delicate nail.

"When a chapter is done, it is done—you turn the page." He suited the action to the words and brought his palm down upon the book. "You understand?" Meg nodded. "You begin another chapter—the first chapter of your life is finished—you understand?" Again Meg nodded. "It was an ugly chapter—it remains with you to make the next chapter a better and a finer one."

"I will not talk of anybody or of anything; but I will always think of one person," persisted Meg, intent upon making the conditions of the bargain clear between her and this stranger.

"I cannot dictate to your thoughts," he replied. "I want you to promise not to speak about the past. What will you say when you are questioned concerning it by teachers, schoolfellows, or servants?"

"I'll tell them it's none of their business, that's what I will tell them," said Meg, with spirit and a relapse into a pronunciation that savored more of Mrs. Browne's than of Mr. Standish's influence.

Mr. Fullbloom chuckled, but the old man remained smileless.

"I have nothing more to add; take the child away," he said.

Mr. Fullbloom put out his hand to Meg. She hesitated, looking toward the old gentleman to say good-by.

Once more the child encountered a glance that seemed to freeze her with its mysterious dislike and she went out in silence.

CHAPTER VI.

MISS REEVES' ESTABLISHMENT FOR YOUNG LADIES.

Moorhouse was a red brick mansion of Elizabethan architecture, standing on the outskirts of the old-fashioned town of Greyling, nestling under a misty embattlement of distant downs. Tracts of ferny solitudes and clumps of woodland lay beyond, cloven by the long straight road that led Londonward. It was difficult to imagine that such rural peacefulness could be found at thirty miles distance from the big metropolis.

Moorhouse was a boarding-school for young ladies. It had gained a high reputation under the direction of its present head-mistress, Miss Reeves, a middle-aged lady of dignified appearance.

It was to Moorhouse Mr. Fullbloom was taking Meg. The child had never gone on a railway journey. The shriek and whistle of the engine as the train dashed along startled her. She felt whirled forward as by a demoniac force, and the pant of the engine seemed to her like the audible heart-beat of some dread monster. She sat rigid and silent in the corner by the window as she passed out of the station across the bridge-spanned river, past squalid streets and roofs crowding below. At last she emerged into more airy and peaceful surroundings. The speed and pant still filled the limpid daylight with terror; but Meg fought against her unstrung nerves and compelled herself to look out of the window. She was passing through a pageantry of meadows lying in the mild sunshine of the March afternoon; of cows grazing, of a pallid golden light in the sky, veiled with fleecy purple clouds. She heard the passing chirp of birds; she caught glimpses of leafless woods spreading a tracery of boughs against the brightness of the sky. There were banks flickering with suggestions of primroses under the hedges; undulating greenswards losing themselves in blue distances. Through the terror of that ride the influence of nature brought comfort to her heart. An exhilarating sense that she was traveling to a better land overcame fear. A house in the distance, perched on a height, with the sunlight on its windows, appeared to her a type of that school to which she was journeying; a sort of magic academy where she would grow worthy of becoming Mr. Standish's friend.

Mr. Fullbloom coughed and Meg turned her head. She caught the amused glance of her traveling companion fixed upon her. The solicitor had been dividing his attention between his paper and the child by his side. Meg had been unconscious of his investigation.

"Reach the school soon now," said the lawyer with his accustomed airy nod.

"I am glad of it," replied Meg.

"Want to be a learned little lady, eh?"

"Yes, that is just what I want to be," Meg answered in an eager tone; "learned as a lady."

"Well, so you will be—excellent school that of Miss Reeves—learn to dance, play the piano, to speak French, German—any amount of accomplishments. Bless me, there will be no talking to you in a year or two. Have to study hard, though."

Meg nodded in token of her readiness to face any amount of study.

"Don't forget your name—Beecham—it is not Browne. Madam was not your mother, or for the matter of that any relation," said the lawyer.

"I knew she was not my mother," said Meg in a low voice.

"No, indeed; light and darkness could not be more unlike."

"You knew my mother?" cried Meg, a flush kindling her cheeks.

"I knew her a little," replied the lawyer guardedly. "You are like her about the mouth and eyes."

"I am not a bit like her," Meg answered in a tone of offense. "She was beautiful—like an angel."

"Yes, she was beautiful," acquiesced Mr. Fullbloom.

Meg looked at the lawyer with a new expression. A halo surrounded his brow, for he had seen her mother.

"Did the old gentleman I saw to-day know her too?" she asked softly.

The lawyer put up his finger and wagged his head.

"Little girls must not ask questions. They must be seen, not heard," he replied, taking up his paper and growing absorbed in its contents.

He did not speak again until the train shortly after stopped at Greyling station.

Before long they had reached Moorhouse, and the door had opened for Meg. As she passed through the portal of the red brick mansion she felt as if she stood upon the threshold of a sanctuary. This sense deepened when, a few moments later, she was confronted by a majestic lady, whom the lawyer introduced to her as Miss Reeves, who looked at her kindly and scrutinizingly. After a low-voiced colloquy with Mr. Fullbloom at the other end of the room, Miss Reeves took her by the hand, saying:

"Your guardian has confided you to my care. I hope, my dear child, that we may both learn soon to love and trust each other."

Meg took with confidence the extended hand. Shortly after, Mr. Fullbloom bade her an airy farewell, and she followed Miss Reeves into a room where a meal was going on.

"Miss Grantley and Madame Vallaria," said the head-mistress addressing the two ladies sitting at either end of the table, "let me introduce to you a new pupil, and to you, young ladies, a new school-fellow—Miss Margaret Beecham. Ursula Grey, let her sit beside you; look after her, she is a stranger."

The room swam around Meg as she took her seat near a girl with a pleasant rosy face and bright eyes shining behind a pair of clever-looking spectacles. The child fancied she detected muffled exclamations, and that on all sides a stare was turned upon her which was not friendly.

The young ladies appeared to her beautifully dressed. They wore pretty brooches and necklaces of colored beads; their shining hair fell about their necks, and they had delicate bits of lace round their throats and wrists. One girl appeared to Meg so beautiful that she forgot everything in the delight of looking at her.

She was roused by a nudge of the elbow.

"Miss Grantley is speaking to you," said her spectacled neighbor. The young lady's lips were quivering with restrained smiles.

"Miss Beecham, will you take a glass of milk or a cup of cocoa?" said the lady at the head of the table.

Meg looked blankly in the direction of the speaker.

"Is not your name Beecham?" said this lady with a shade of annoyance in her voice.

Meg shook her head in the negative; then suddenly remembering the warning she had received not to forget:

"Yes—Beecham—that's my name," she said hurriedly, with the vivid nod that usually accompanied her assertions.

A titter went round the table.

"Hush!" said Miss Grantley severely.

Meg sat stiff and upright.

"Will you have milk or cocoa?" repeated Miss Grantley.

"Cocoa," blurted out Meg with monosyllabic brevity, in her confusion forgetting her manners.

She was intensely aware of the nudgings going on around her; of subdued fits of laughter shaking some of the young ladies; of the surprised stare of others. She caught Miss Grantley's cold glance.

Meg seized with both hands the cup passed on to her and hurriedly gulped down some of its contents.

As she put it down she again encountered shocked and amazed glances. An embarrassed misgiving fell upon her. Breaking her bread into small morsels she slowly munched, gazing down into her plate.

When she became aware of a general pushing back of chairs and of rising about her, Meg stood up. She knew the teacher was saying grace. Her spectacled neighbor then nodded.

"Come along," she said, and Meg followed.

The girls were pouring into another room. They at once surrounded Meg. The whispers became audible.

"Who is she?"

"Who brought her?"

"Where did she come from?"

To Meg's surprise, one of the girls approached her and said with familiar cordiality:

"What is your name—your real name, I mean?"

"My real name?" repeated Meg. She was standing inflexibly upright near a table.

"The name you were called by before to-day?" said her interrogator.

"You did not recognize your name when you were called Beecham—what is your real name?" said another.

Meg did not answer for a moment. She remembered her promise to the mysterious white-haired stranger. Then she said huskily:

"What does it signify what name I had before?"

Again she paused.

"Then you had another name?" said the pretty girl in a thin, high voice. "How very romantic!"

"Don't tease her—what does it signify?" put in Ursula.

"What does it signify?" was repeated all round in what Meg fancied a not unkindly tone. She took courage.

"What is in a name?" demanded one of the girls.

"A rose by any other name would smell as sweet would it not?" said another.

"Yes," said Meg, bewildered.

"Where did you live!" questioned one.

Meg remained mute. Again her promise to the mysterious stranger sealed her lips.

"Up a tree," suggested one.

"Second branch," said another with a laugh.

"Letters to you came addressed 'Miss What's-her-name, second branch, fourth tree, on the right side of the road,'" cried a third.

This description of Meg's late abode was greeted by peals of laughter.

"Visitors climbed up," suggested another.

"Why do you say those things?" asked Meg, looking round on the laughing faces. "I am come here to learn lessons—to grow up to be a lady. That's what I come for."

"A lady!" echoed all around her.

"A lady is born a lady," said a tall girl who had not spoken hitherto. She had a high nose and a voice of ice.

"My mother was a lady," said Meg.

"Your mother!" was echoed all around.

Meg did not answer; words seemed to tremble on her lips as she gazed on her tormentors.

"Is your dress her taste?" asked one.

"Did she teach you to say 'Cocoa' like that, without saying 'if you please'?" asked another, mimicking Meg's answer to Miss Grantley.

"My mother taught me nothing—she is dead," said Meg slowly.

There was a pause.

Then the tormentors began again.

"Are you sure you would know a lady if you saw one?"

"Would you call the grocer's wife a lady because she wears a silk dress?" demanded the Roman-nosed young lady in her chilly voice.

"No," said Meg with concentration.

"Does a lady go about playing the street-organ?" asked a fat, stupid-faced girl.

"No," again said Meg fiercely. Then addressing the assembly generally, but looking especially at the high-nosed young lady, she went on: "Why do you want to know all those things about me? It's idle curiosity—that's what I call it. And if my dress is ugly, what is that to you? I come here to learn lessons and to be a lady."

"But do you know what it is to be a lady?" replied the girl.

"One is born, not made a lady," said another.

"If," said Meg, trembling with energy, looking round on her persecutors, "to be a born lady makes one laugh at another because she's badly dressed, and to mock her because she's not got fine manners, then to be a born lady is to be vulgar and cruel—that's what I think."

For a moment there was silence; then the stupid-looking girl, coming close to Meg and thrusting her face near hers, said in a jeering drawl:

"I saw you and your mother selling matches in Bond Street last Easter holidays. Your mother had a red handkerchief round her head and a monkey under her arm."

"That is a falsehood!" said Meg. Up flashed the little brown hand and came down with a slap on the dull, mocking face.

There was a hubbub.

Cries of "She's a savage!" "A gypsy!"

"We will tell Miss Reeves," was vociferated on all sides.

Above the tumult rose the voice of Ursula:

"You deserved that slap, Laura Harris. Miss Beecham had told us her mother was dead. She has been teased too much."

A bell sounded and the head-mistress, followed by the other teachers and the servants, entered the room.

"Silence, young ladies," said Miss Reeves.

Prayer-time had come at Moorhouse.

CHAPTER VII.

AT SCHOOL.

Meg was going through the ordeal that her friend had set for her, and she strung herself to endurance. She felt she was tabooed by these fashionable young ladies, and she fiercely anticipated their neglect. She avoided them; she rejected Ursula's advances with impatience.

For awhile some of the girls felt a temptation to bait this little badger, but at last either the freshness or the excitement of the sport died away. Perhaps, too, a certain amount of fear restrained them. The slap administered to Laura Harris had made an impression, and it was considered advisable not to goad the "savage" beyond bounds. Meg after awhile was very much left alone.

She was an outcast, and she felt homesick for the London cage from which she had flitted, and which the presence of a friend had cheered. For the first time, also, she realized her ignorance, and with resolute heroism she set herself to learn. She worked with astonishing zeal. At her books and lessons Meg did not feel so lonely. At church and in her walks through the pleasant country lanes the sense of her absolute isolation was lifted. In recreation hours she sat apart from her schoolfellows. There was a yew tree on the outskirts of the playground into which she climbed to read Goldsmith's "Animated Nature." She began its perusal for the sake of the donor; then, gradually, this book of wonder fascinated her. The description it gave of strange, beautiful creatures, of birds especially, enthralled her. She gathered from the pages hints of far-away countries that called to her like a voice. This little town-bred heart was seized with a passionate love of nature and a foolish love of wild flowers. As she formed one of the regiment of girls who tramped, two and two, through the country lanes, the beauty of nature seemed to comfort Meg as if the touch of a reassuring hand were laid upon her heart. She would almost forget, then, that she was an object of mockery or patronage to her fellows. In the beautiful old church she felt nearly happy. "I am out of school," she would say to herself. The voice of the organ took her immensely. It seemed to be a voice talking to God. She liked the clergyman also. He was an old gentleman who appeared to her to be endowed with great benevolence. She thought his sermons marvels of eloquence. When, in answer to her long stare, his eye sometimes rested upon her, she felt immensely distinguished and honored.

The teachers of Moorhouse were as much puzzled concerning Meg as were the girls. She knew so much of some subjects and so little of others. Miss Reeves, after a careful examination of the new pupil's acquirements, declared that Meg might beat the girls of the upper class in knowledge of some parts of history, and in familiarity with some of Shakespeare's plays; while the lower classes might overmaster her in the elements of arithmetic, geography, and other subjects.

Mr. Foster, the arithmetic master, a lank man with a large nose and a long neck, who looked like an innocent vulture, and who had never been known to give a bad mark, contenting himself with feebly rubbing out the mistakes on the slates presented to him, was bewildered by Meg's absolute ignorance of the rules of arithmetic, and by her dependence upon her fingers for counters.

"Miss Beecham is a *table-rase*, as was the great philosopher Descartes before he began to observe for the sake of his method," said the professor to Miss Reeves, with forefinger uplifted, for Mr. Foster was proud of making little pedantic jokes.

Madame Vallaria, the middle-aged lady who superintended the music of the establishment, teaching piano and singing from morning till night, was divided between admiration for Meg's correct ear and determination to learn, and despair over the stiffness of her fingers and her ignorance of the first elements of music. The signora was hot-tempered; her nerves were jarred by listening to incessant practice.

"No, no, it is impossible! I will not teach you—I will refuse—I will say to Miss Reeves that I cannot!" She sometimes exclaimed, addressing Meg: "Your fingers are like the chop sticks the Chinese do use for eating. You thump—thump—thump! I hear it in my sleep. It ever gives me the nightmare." Sometimes Mme. Vallaria relented and with voluble heartiness would exclaim: "Oh, Povera! your leetle heart is set to learn; you are so courageous; and your ear it is exact, like a machine made to catch the sounds. Yes, I will teach you—you shall learn it yet—the piano—never fear!"

Mr. Eyre, the shy and eminent professor who came down twice a week from London to take classes of history and English literature of younger and elder pupils, would alternately pass from delight to annoyance at Meg's answers. Her indifference to dates appeared to him a sort of moral deficiency—it amounted to contempt. Her power of realizing historical facts and characters in which she took an interest was vivid, as if she had been a spectator of the events described, and had a personal acquaintance with the actors therein. He vowed she spoke of Julius Cæsar as if she knew him, and of his murder as if it had happened yesterday and was the subject of a leader in this morning's *Times*. He was appalled and puzzled, he exhorted, he raged; but his eye rested expectantly upon Meg when her companions floundered behind, and the dullness of the class was relieved for him by the audacity of her answers.

"You ought to go up to London to see the coronation," he said to her one day when the theme of the lesson was Queen Elizabeth's reign, and Meg surpassed herself in the brilliancy of her descriptive replies and the astounding incorrectness of her dates.

"What coronation?" asked Meg.

"That of Queen Elizabeth."

"But she is dead and buried in Westminster Abbey," Meg rejoined blankly, being dismally dense in apprehending a joke.

"Is she?" replied Mr. Eyre with feigned astonishment, and as was his wont when he bantered his pupils, he set about biting what remained of his nails and scribbled the lessons to be learned in the following week.

"Let her go on! She will go forever and ever backward till she is stopped by the pyramid of Ghizeh!" he remarked another day as Meg placed the date of Cromwell a century too early, and was sending it back another hundred years when she found she was wrong.

Miss Grantley, the English and geography teacher to the younger class, was antagonistically chilly in her treatment of Meg. The child felt she was disliked, and with that precise and unsympathetic teacher her deficiencies came out flagrantly. Signora Vallaria's voluble wailings, Dr. Grey's jokes, did not dispirit Meg as did Miss Grantley's frosty censoriousness.

Meg was solitary, and in her solitude she grew defiant and repellent. Her heart suffered from the atmosphere of repression. As far as outward appearances went she resembled her comrades; she was dressed like her fellow-pupils, her wardrobe having been replenished under Miss Reeves' direction; but inwardly she was not of them. She sat among them like an owl among sparrows.

She observed them. As she had watched the hubbub of the lodging-house, so she now watched the routine of the school. The girls of the first class, tall, elegantly dressed, appeared to her like young goddesses.

Some of those nodded to her kindly as they passed, and she returned the salute awkwardly without a smile.

Among the girls who had tormented her on her first night, a group, headed by Miss Rosamond Pinkett, the cold-eyed, straight-backed, Roman-nosed young lady, kept up an aggressive attitude. It still appeared to Miss Pinkett that a degradation had been inflicted on the school by the introduction of the "savage," and she ignored Meg with contemptuous coldness. This young lady's bosom friend, Gwendoline Lister, the beauty of the school, had a nature addicted to romance. Her mind was like a story-book in which every page contained a thrilling incident of which she was usually the heroine.

The sudden appearance of Meg, in a costume that suggested the dress of a poor tradesman's child, her fierce refusal to betray anything concerning her antecedents except the reiteration that her mother was a lady, fired the beauty's fancy. Meg, she imagined, was the scion of a noble family, stolen by gypsies, found at last, and sent here to be educated.

"Daughter of a ballet-dancer, my dear, you mean," Miss Pinkett said with an icy sniff. "That ridiculous drawing speaks volumes."

The drawing to which Miss Pinkett alluded, and from which the Beauty had evolved her romance, was an attempt made by Meg to repeat from memory that dear fashion plate, which she had given away.

She had rudely drawn a small-mouthed, large-eyed face, the head wreathed with roses, the dress covered with roses. Underneath she had written in Roman characters, "My mother." This drawing had been found in Goldsmith's "Animated Nature," taken out by prying fingers, and had been passed from hand to hand. Where others had found food for mockery, Miss Lister had found food for her imagination.

Meg had come on the scene as Miss Pinkett was in the act of examining the sketch. With a cry she had snatched it out of the enemy's grasp, and, tearing it to bits, she had flung herself from the presence of the girls.

Ursula continued the defense of the stranger, and made advances to Meg, which the child persistently refused.

"Why won't you take my sweets?" Ursula asked once in a piqued tone.

"I don't want them," said Meg with jerky abruptness.

"Why? Is it because you have none to give in return?" demanded Ursula bluntly.

"I don't want them—that is all!" answered Meg.

"It is pride—nothing but pride!" said Ursula, turning away with a displeased gleam of her spectacles.

A few days later an incident happened which showed that Meg was not all indifferent to kindness. The spring had come and decked with lavish waste of blossoms disgraced corners as well as more favored places. It had rimmed with a fringe of velvet wallflower the top of the arid garden wall. The orange and brown blooms spread in the sunlight, swayed in the breeze, attracted the murmuring bees, and sang the praise of spring in delicate wafts of perfume.

"How delicious those wallflowers smell," said Ursula, sniffing the air with head thrown back. "It is a shame they should be unpluckable. I wish I had a handful."

Meg heard the wish as she sat perched on the yew tree. When Ursula turned away she abandoned her leafy throne, and swung herself from one of the branches on to the trellis that covered the wall. It was a high wall, but she climbed it with the precision of a woodland animal, here grasping the trellis, there planting her foot on some bit of projecting masonry. "You'll fall!" cried a chorus of voices. "To climb that wall is absolutely forbidden, Miss Beecham," called out Miss Pinkett's voice. "I will go and tell Miss Grantley," cried Laura Harris, setting off at a run. Meg, undismayed by warnings and threats, pursued her quest.

A moment later Ursula felt a gentle touch on the elbow, and a fragrant bunch of brown blossoms was thrust into her hand.

"Meg, you did not!" she cried with amazed spectacles, gazing at the child, who bore marks of her recent encounter with the perils of the wall.

Meg nodded.

Ursula buried her nose into the flowers with a hesitating expression as Miss Grantley came up, followed by girls.

"Miss Beecham, go indoors at once! You shall stay in this afternoon for this unlady-like and disobedient conduct. Ursula, those flowers must be given up!"

MEG PULLS THE FORBIDDEN FLOWERS.—Page 94.

Meg went indoors without a murmur, and zealously devoted herself to the task set her as expiation of her offense. She took pleasure in its difficulty. She was glad the day was so beautiful, that the room was full of sunshine, and the wandering puffs of wind brought in messages from the odorous sweetness of the day. She was proud of being punished for Ursula's sake. It seemed to put her on a more equal footing, as if repaying her for past kindness.

Another incident that followed shortly after the wall-climbing episode proved that Meg's sense of loyalty survived amid the withering influence of loveless criticisms around her.

Miss Gwendoline Lister, because of her beauty, was a personality in the school. She suffered the penalties of celebrity. Stories were current concerning her. One averred that she had been found dissolved in tears on the discovery of a freckle upon her nose. Another rumor was current that the Beauty spent the afternoon of wet half-holidays locked up in the room she and Miss Pinkett shared in common arranging and dressing her hair in various fashions, enhancing her charms with rouge and powder, and trying on her ball dress.

Perhaps this report arose from the fact of a rouge pot having been found in the school. Some averred it was the property of Miss Lister, others declared its contents had been used by the young ladies who had taken part in a theatrical entertainment given on the occasion of breaking up for the holidays.

Meg, in her isolation, took no interest in the "rouge pot controversy." One afternoon, to her surprise, she was beckoned by Miss Pinkett into the room shared by her and Gwendoline.

The Beauty was standing near the dressing-table, a radiant vision clothed in white, with hair unbound, wreathed with roses, and with roses in the bodice of her dress.

For a moment Meg remained struck dumb with admiration, then came a sudden revolution. In her wide experience of life in the boarding-house she had known an obscure member of the theatrical profession. This little slip of the foot lights, who spent her life in alternate squalor and fairy-like splendor, had on one or two occasions dressed herself up for Meg's benefit. The child had grown to know cheeks bedabbled with paint and eyes outlined with bismuth. The face of Miss Lister brought back this acquaintance of bygone times.

"Well, what do I look like?" said Gwendoline, with her head cocked on one side and her finger-tips caressing the roses in her bodice. "You know, little monkey, you are not to tell."

Miss Pinkett watched the effect on Meg with cold curiosity.

"You look much prettier as you are every day," said Meg.

"Do I look like your mother?"

"My mother!" repeated the child, and she began to tremble.

"I copied the portrait you drew, roses and all," said the Beauty.

"My mother never painted her cheeks; she never put black under her eyes. You are like a Christy minstrel painted pink and white—that's what you are like!" said Meg, with the concentration of fury in her voice. She turned, unlocked the door, and slammed it behind her.

As she emerged out of the room the dressing bell for tea rang, and she encountered a group of girls waiting outside. They cried breathlessly:

"What are they doing inside?"

"Is not Gwendoline dressing up? Does she rouge her cheeks?"

"I saw a bit of a white dress."

"I did—I did! Tell us, Meg—Meg!"

But Meg did not answer. She tore along the passage and up the stairs till she came to a solitary attic. She flung herself down on the floor and hammered the insensate boards with her fists. In her untamed heart she would have wished to wipe the insult from her mother's memory by thus maltreating the painted cheeks of Miss Lister.

When the tea bell rang Meg went downstairs.

"Where are Miss Pinkett and Miss Lister?" asked Miss Reeves, after she had said grace, glancing down the table.

"They have not come down yet from their room, madam," said the attending parlor-maid.

"Miss Lister is dressing up. Miss Beecham was there—she knows," said Laura Harris, who might be relied upon for giving information on the doings of the other girls.

"Miss Beecham knows!" repeated some other voices.

"Miss Lister puts paint on her cheeks," resumed Laura, growing more explicit.

"I hope not!" said Miss Reeves, with an anxious brow, and her eye rested upon Meg.

"I heard it said before by Miss Reeves' young laidees," put in Signora Vallaria, rolling her dark eyes. "Tell, my leetle Meg, what they were doing, the silly young laidees, when they call you in?"

At this moment Miss Pinkett and Gwendoline entered. The Beauty's face was shining with soap.

"What were you doing in your room, young ladies?" asked Miss Reeves gravely.

"I suppose, madam, Miss Beecham has been telling," replied Miss Pinkett.

"No, we are waiting for her answer to the question I have just put to you."

Meg was conscious of every eye being turned upon her—Miss Reeves sternly questioning, Miss Pinkett coldly supercilious, Gwendoline, with pursed lips, imploring. She stood up, her little red lips closed tightly, her heart fiercely divided between a desire for vengeance and a sense of loyalty. After a pause she said:

"They called me into the room to make fun of a portrait of my mother which I had drawn."

A murmur of comical disappointment from the girls round the table, an expression of relief on the faces of the two culprits, greeted this answer.

"It was such an absurd portrait, madam," said Miss Pinkett in an explanatory tone; "a lady suffering from the mumps wearing a wreath of roses."

A titter went round the table.

"Hush!" said Miss Reeves seriously. "It is unkind to laugh at the child. Sit down, young ladies."

"It was awfully good of you, Meg, not to tell about me," said Gwendoline that evening, when she got Meg alone. "I am awfully obliged. I am sorry I offended you. Will you forgive me?"

"No!" said Meg emphatically, turning her back upon the Beauty and walking stiffly away.

CHAPTER VIII.

THE SCHOOL ANNUAL.

Ursula had founded the "Moorhouse Annual." The volume appeared every year just before the midsummer holidays. It consisted of poems and stories by the young ladies, copied in Miss Clara Maxton's beautiful copperplate writing, and edited by Ursula.

Ursula was editress, illustrator, and chief contributor. The history of the courtship, squabbles, friendships, and adventures of Mr. Gander and Miss Chilblane, chiefly related in pen-and-ink drawings, with commentaries appended beneath, by Ursula, was a leading feature of the periodical.

The would-be contributors to the annual usually assembled some Saturday afternoon in May, to read aloud their MSS. and submit them to the editorial judgment.

The important Saturday had arrived, and Ursula and her staff were assembled, with Miss Reeves' permission, in the smaller schoolroom. Ursula sat at the head of the table in an impressive armchair; the spectacles astride her *retroussé* nose seemed critically brilliant.

Meg slunk in, and sat at the window within earshot.

Gwendoline had asked her on entering, MS. in hand, if she was going to read a story. "I am sure you could write a most bewitching story about that beautiful lady," the Beauty had averred.

"No, no, no!" said Meg, retreating into the veranda.

She had crept back in time to hear Laura Harris read her tale. It appeared to be the history of a confectioner, who owned a famous west-end shop, which was in vogue with the fashionable and wealthy. Ladies sat there and feasted. The description of its charms had apparently such an overwhelming attraction for the authoress that she could not prevail on her pen to quit it and pass on with her story. There was a gigantic wedding-cake, with a sugar-almond top, fully a yard high. The cream puffs, the jam tarts, the ices, the chocolates, the sweets were piled on with profusion.

The conclusion of this story was not arrived at.

Ursula rapped the table with her paper-knife.

"Story declined with thanks," she said briefly.

"Why?" asked Laura indignantly.

"Because, notwithstanding the delicious cakes, we consider it in bad taste," replied Ursula, using the editorial "we" with fine effect.

"Miss Grant, have you a story to submit to us for the forthcoming annual?"

Miss Grant had made a hit the year before by her story of "The Ghostly Postman," who knocked in the ordinary way, and sent summons of death by the letter box.

An audible shiver ran through the audience as she now unrolled her MS., and in a deep voice read the title—"The Midnight Yell."

The story told of a beautiful country house, on a moor, in which there was a haunted chamber. Whoever entered that room at night never came out alive. At midnight a yell would ring through the mansion—unearthly, blood curdling. When the chamber was broken into the guest was always found dead, with arms outstretched and eyes starting out of their sockets. Who uttered that midnight yell?—was it the living or the dead? The visitor or the ghost? None could tell. Some said it was an old hag who haunted the chamber, some said it was a beautiful white lady; but it was generally reported to be a murdered queen.

A sigh greeted this story.

"Accepted," said Ursula, in a business-like tone.

"Will it be illustrated?" inquired the authoress anxiously.

"Yes; probably with a spectral donkey braying," said Ursula.

"Oh, no, I cannot allow that!" said the authoress.

"We decline to hold communications about the MSS., refused or accepted," replied Ursula, bringing her paper-knife sharply down upon the table.

"Miss Lister's story," she demanded.

"It is entitled," said Gwendoline in a falsetto voice, "'The Lover's Grave.'" The Beauty proceeded to read how a gypsy with weird, mystic, somber eyes, and serpent-like, coiling, blue-black hair, had scanned the shell-like palm of a lovely Venetian maiden with golden tresses, and warned her with strange fatal mutterings that to her love and death would come hand in hand. Careless of the muttered prophecy, the Venetian damsel with hair like bullion, and clad in a rich violet velvet gown, and with a necklace of pearls clasped about her lily-white throat, set off every morning in her gondola to look for the gallant whom she could love. One day the predicted lover came in another gondola; he was beautiful as Apollo. His mustache was long and silky, his eyes liquid and violet; he had an air of combined tenderness and strength. The gondolas drifted toward each other, impelled by fate. The lady rose impulsively; so did the gentleman. They endeavored to embrace. As they did so, both fell into the water. For awhile they floated on the blue-green flood, smiling seraphically at each other, then they subsided gracefully, and were drowned, and ever after that spot was called "The Lovers' Grave."

"It will make a pretty picture," said Ursula. "I can see the two drowning with that set seraphic smile, as if they liked it."

"Yes," said Gwendoline, who never saw a joke, "it will make a lovely picture." "I have written a poem," said Miss Blanche Hathers modestly, taking out a roll of paper tied with bows of pink satin ribbon.
A hum of approbation greeted this announcement.
"Go on," said Ursula, with the freezing brevity of the editor.
"The poem is called 'A Lament,' perhaps it might be more appropriately called 'A Deserted Maiden's Prayer.'"
Ursula nodded. Miss Hathers began effectively:
"Oh! star of even
My heart is riven,
Come thou down and shine
In these eyes of mine;
'Twill draw him back."
Ursula, forgetting editorial dignity, completed the couplet, amid giggles and laughter:
"And his cheek I'll smack."
The discomfited poetess folded up her effusion. The next line was:
"On dreamy track,"
and it was only the first verse.
"'Twill draw him back,
On dreamy track."
she repeated in an injured voice.
"Never mind on what track—we must shunt him," said Ursula with decision.
"Any more MSS.?" she inquired, scanning the assembled contributors.

There came a rustle of many pages.

Miss Margaret Smith submitted the story of "The First Ball-dress," which had a high moral; it was accepted, and was voted lovely. Miss Sarah Robbins contributed "The Vampire Schoolmistress," an awful tale of a teacher, whose pupils all died mysteriously—"sucked like oranges," Ursula suggested. One young lady gave an account of her trip to Paris, which contained vivid descriptions of bonnets and capes, and some obscure allusions to the galleries.

"My story is entitled 'The Noble Heiress,'" said Miss Pinkett. In a lisping, fine voice the young lady read the story of a wealthy damsel, who lived in a beautiful house, exquisitely furnished.

As Portia was at Belmont, so was this heiress sought in marriage by many suitors. It was said that besides her wealth she possessed "love-powders;" for all who saw her loved her. But she was as sensible as she was rich and beautiful, and she kept her heart in check. It was only when the eldest son of a marquis came forward to woo her that she allowed herself to love. Wealth and nobility, the sensible heiress felt, was the true marriage sung of by poets from all ages. The wedding presents were numerous—the author was lavish in descriptions of the diamonds, the rubies, the emeralds. The wedding-dress was a charming costume, which Miss Pinkett described with much fervor.

Meg, who had sat still all the time with her chin in her hands, like a surly little exile from the circle, looked as if the foolish tales irritated her. Suddenly, in a clear, abrupt voice she said:

"Shall I tell you my story?"

"Your story?" echoed the girls, amazed.

"Yes," said Ursula.

"Do!" exclaimed Gwendoline.

"It is the story of a toad," said Meg.

"Of a toad!" repeated Gwendoline in dismay.

"There was once upon a time a toad," Meg began, breathing heavily—taking no notice of the interruption.

"It was ugly, lonely, and always in danger of being kicked and crushed; but it had splendid eyes, like jewels. At night it liked to crawl out and look up at the beautiful stars. Every one who saw it," Meg went on with more concentration, "looked at it with disgust. The toad used to make its way to the edge of the still water and look at itself, and think 'how they hate me.' It envied the frogs which croaked and could jump, while it could only crawl.

"Down in the water below the ground lived the great mother of all the toads, and this little toad went down to find her, for it wished to ask her why it had ever been born? The mother of all the toads was immensely large. She had bigger and more beautiful eyes than any other toad. They were like soft precious stones, and round each eye was a circle of light like a ring of gold. The little toad sat before her and said:

"'Why have I been born? Why should I be crushed and beaten, and looked at with disgust? Why do the children put out their little red lips at me? They hate and fear me. Sometimes when they see me they step back and go headlong into the water. I have not even power to punish them.'

"And the mother of all the toads did not answer, she only blinked. She showed no sympathy at all, and never looked at the little toad.

"Once the toad thought it would do a kind thing. It lived near a garden, and in it there was a child who had a pet flower, and when the child went away the toad took care of the flower, brought water to it, scratched the earth, and took all the insects away.

"When the child returned the flower was more beautiful than before. But when it saw the toad, it stamped its little foot, crying 'Kill it! kill it!' and the gardener gave the poor toad a kick with his nailed boot on its tender side, and threw it, almost killed, into the water. So the little toad said 'I will never like anybody again, and I will never do a kind thing.'

"Its heart grew wicked." Meg put emphasis on this last word. "It had teeth to bite, it croaked its ugliest, and it had just one longing to see something uglier than itself. One day it saw this thing. It was a pug dog—petted, and fed, and caressed, and wearing a gold collar round its neck. The toad was glad there was something uglier than itself; it frightened the pug dog, and was comforted.

"One day as the little toad was crawling along it heard steps. 'I shall be killed it said,' and it tried to hurry away. But the steps came nearer and nearer. Suddenly the toad felt itself taken up gently, and it saw bending over it the face of a young man, and it was a kind face; and the young man put the little toad down in a sheltered spot, saying 'Remain there, out of harm's way, till I come back.' He went away." Here Meg's voice faltered.

"He did not know that there were dreadful thorns in that spot; but the little toad tried for the sake of that friend not to mind. It remained there, and it was always listening for the young man's steps coming back. That is all," said Meg in abrupt conclusion.

There was a silence.

Then Miss Pinkett said: "What a shocking story!"

"Shocking!" circled round the table.

"Were you the little toad?" asked Laura Harris.

"Yes!" said Meg curtly.

"I like that story," said Ursula, "and I shall draw such a toad."

CHAPTER IX.

DRIFTING AWAY.

It was the eve of the midsummer holidays; the examinations were over. Miss Pinkett had come out victorious in music and geography, Ursula in drawing and artistic needlework. The Beauty had proved to be nowhere in the competition. Meg had taken no prize, but she had been encouraged by kind reports from Signora Vallaria and Mr. Eyre. She had worked incessantly, and some of the teachers had recognized her zeal.

The tension of the past few weeks was relaxed, and Miss Reeves was giving the picnic that she usually organized for her pupils, in the Surrey woods, watered by a branch of the Thames. It was a perfect summer day, broadly golden, benignly calm.

The repast under the trees was over; the girls, tired of their games, sat about in groups discussing plans for the holidays. Meg sat apart. In the midst of the surrounding gayety the loneliness of her heart deepened. She was enduring the tantalizing pangs of picturing the happy hours from which she was excluded.

She heard of the dear little children who would come to the station to welcome these home-comers; of the lawn-tennis parties, the rides, the picnics which awaited them. One girl was going home for the wedding of her sister; another was promised a pony to ride out with her brother George. There were vivid descriptions going on all around her of the charms of holidays. Oh, the delights of not hearing the school-bell of a morning—of awaking at the appointed hour, and being able to turn round cosily for another sleep! All were going home; even the teachers looked forward to meeting relatives and friends. She alone was remaining—she alone of all the school had no home to go to. She rose and wandered away. Her desolate little heart could bear it no more: a bitter sense was growing there that no one cared for her— that if Mr. Standish cared for her he would have written.

Meg walked away, not minding where she went, willing only to be out of earshot of that joyous talk. She presently found herself by the river's bank; and there, moored among the reeds, was the longboat hired for the occasion, in which the girls had rowed each other in parties all the morning.

Ursula had pressed her to join the group of which she was a member, but Meg had refused. It had seemed to the child enough to lie among the ferns, inhaling the delicate, pungent perfumes, feeling the breath of the summer day on her cheek, surrendering herself to the strength and calm of nature's influence.

Meg now stepped into the boat and sat down. It was like being in a cradle, she thought, as the water softly rocked the craft. No one was near. Presently she perceived that the boat was sliding off—softly, softly the shore was receding; the banks and the long reeds were falling back.

Meg watched immobile. Bundles of oars lay at the bottom of the boat; which was also strewn with bunches of meadow-sweet, elder-blossoms, forget-me-nots, and other riverside trophies which the girls had plucked on their travels. Meg sat upright like a startled rabbit, wondering when the boat would stop. She wished that it would never stop—that it would carry her away, away, she knew not whither! She had heard the girls speak of the "weir." What was that? Was it some weird spot?—a strange island, perhaps, inhabited by some of the water-fowl of which she had read?

Then she perceived that the boat had swung itself round; it was drifting down with the current. The river was narrow, and there was not another boat within sight. Without oars, without sails, without guidance, the little craft was making its way, keeping right in the middle of the stream. For a moment Meg could not believe; then joy seized her—she was off on her travels!

Past pale-green willows that hung their branches down into the water, filling it with a twilight of green, sprinkling its surface with leaves as with a goblin fleet; past sunny, silent stretches of woodland and meadows where cows grazed and looked at her with horny heads sharply outlined against the light; past banks full of flowers went Meg. The sun shone for her, the breeze stirred for her, the trees seemed to look at her. She felt like a little river-queen.

As she drifted along, the misery and loneliness at her heart dropped, like the leaves the breeze had shaken from the willows. She, the despised Meg, was free; all nature was her playfellow. From the banks the cuckoo cried like a friendly presence playing at "hide-and-seek" with her. A kingfisher, with a breast like a jewel fashioned in the sky, skimmed past her where the solitude was shadiest. From the forked branches of a willow a water hen, sitting on its nest, peered at her with trustful eyes; a water rat from under the leaf of a water lily eyed her with pleasant sympathy, as if he understood the pleasures of a skiff on a summer day. The fishes leaped and made rippled circles around her.

After awhile the river broadened. She passed boathouses that appeared to stand in the water, their roofs bright with flowers; she drifted along a bank where children were playing. They left their games to watch her. They pointed at her, and Meg lifted herself up that she might be better seen, feeling more than ever like a little river queen. She, the wild, despised Meg, was envied and admired!

Once more the river grew lonely. Presently she thought she heard a distant, drowsy sound; it grew louder; the boat seemed to glide along more quickly. After awhile the sound became a roar, and the boat skimmed along as if it were flying; still the water remained smooth as glass. She fancied she heard voices shouting, but the roar of the water filled her ears till it became a boom. She sat up straight and rigid, and as she flashed past she saw with dreadful clearness the word "Danger" written up in great letters on a post by the riverside. For the first time Meg's heart began to beat. She heard shouts; she turned her head, and again she saw with terrible distinctness the word "Danger" written above the place the boat was making for. The water-line ended there, and she understood the booming was the roar of the river rushing down to a lower level. Her boat would upset and she must drown! Meg shut her eyes. Mr. Standish, the old boarding-house, seemed to rise before her as she speeded along.

Suddenly the boat jerked, struggling like a living creature arrested in full flight.

"Don't move!" shouted a voice; and Meg, quiet as an image, felt the struggling boat slowly turned round; a head showed above the water; a muscular arm, bare to the elbow, a figure clad in white flannels, swimming low and strong, were beside her.

It had been accomplished in one moment's time. The boat was being now pushed in the direction of a bank, on which stood a watching group of young men, clad, like her rescuer, in white flannels and loose, bright-colored jackets. One of these got into the water, and catching the prow of the boat, pulled it in with one vigorous sweep. The keel grazed the bottom of the river; the young men lifted Meg and set her on shore.

"Well, if ever a little girl escaped drowning you have!" said her rescuer, giving himself a shake.

Meg was silent as she realized that she had been saved from drowning in the whirl and foam of roaring water. The young men looked at her with kind, smiling glances—she was surrounded with laughing eyes and gleaming teeth. They plied her with questions of "Who was she?" "What was her name?" "Where did she come from?" "Had she been frightened?"

She explained how she had got into the boat and she had drifted away. No, she had not been frightened—only when she saw the word "Danger" she had begun to be afraid.

Her rescuers voted that she was a heroine.

The young men moved away a few steps and held a consultation; one, who had an eyeglass stuck in his eye and a pipe in his mouth, came forward.

"Get into the boat, Meg, and we will all row you back. You will point out the place you came from when we approach it."

He handed Meg in, and the young fellows vied with each other to pay her attention. One put a cushion at her back, another a plank to her feet. "Meg," they vowed, "must be rowed back in triumph."

They stepped into the boat, four took oars. Another sat behind Meg, ropes in hand. Presently they lit their pipes. Meg sat back in state. How kind they were! They were not cross, as girls mostly were; they did not mock or tease her; they did not say a word of what some of the girls called chaff. She watched with amazement all their pipes going puff, puff, puff. She liked them because they did not talk much. They reminded her of Mr. Standish. When their eyes caught hers they gave her a smile. How strong they were! She watched their muscular arms and hands sweeping the water with their oars, the rhythmic movement of their swaying bodies.

No Greek maiden delivered from peril by a group of demi-gods ever felt more lost in dreamy wonder and gratitude than did Meg, rowed up the river by her rescuers. Her eyes rested oftenest on the one who had saved her—he seemed to her the most magnificent member of this gallant crew. He had laughing, twinkling eyes, thick, short, curly hair, silky mustache no bigger than an eyebrow. It occurred to her that she had not thanked him for saving her life. She turned over in her mind what was the proper thing to say. She tried to recollect what persons in story-books said to the saviours of their lives, but she could not remember; she pondered, but the words of gratitude would not come. At last she exclaimed abruptly:

"You saved my life—and—and—I am very much obliged to you."

A peal of laughter taken up by all the group greeted this speech. The laughter was so jovial and good-natured that Meg felt at her ease. It seemed to say: "What nonsense! Don't thank me. It was nothing."

Then they began to question her again: "Was she afraid of meeting her schoolmistress? Would she be scolded?"

Meg admitted the possibility of being scolded. Her rescuers vowed that they would plead for her. They would extract a promise from the schoolmistress not to punish her. Meg must not be scolded; Meg must be welcomed home like the prodigal returning.

"There!" exclaimed Meg dejectedly, pointing to a group of girls and teachers looking up and down the river. She enjoyed the amazement of the spectators as from the bank they watched her triumphant return. With a sweep of the oars the boat came alongside the shore. Miss Reeves stepped forward.

"You must have been frightened, madam, at this young lady's disappearance," said Meg's rescuer, jumping on shore.

Meg allowed herself to be helped out like a princess by the oarsmen.

"We had not long missed the child," replied Miss Reeves. "We were startled when we discovered that the boat was gone. She ought not to have gone alone—it was very thoughtless."

"The boat drifted away with her—it nearly carried her down the weir," said the spokesman. "She was very courageous."

Meg felt herself pleaded for, and listened, motionless.

"You saved her life?" said Miss Reeves.

"I was able, by swimming out in time, to turn the boat's head," replied the young man lightly. "She behaved with great pluck."

"I am most grateful, and I shall acquaint her guardians," said Miss Reeves.

"No, no—pray don't!" replied the young man; and his comrades echoed his words. "Only," he added with a merry twinkle, "do not let Miss Meg be scolded! She is so spirited, so courageous—she ought to have a medal for steadiness of nerves."

Miss Reeves hesitated, then she said smiling: "She will not be scolded."

The announcement was received with approbation, the young men shook hands with Meg, and lifting their white caps to Miss Reeves and the schoolgirls, turned away.

Meg watched their figures retreating through the trees; and when they vanished she felt the loneliness creep over her again.

CHAPTER X.

REBELLION.

The second week of the holidays had come. For close upon a fortnight Meg had been alone with Miss Grantley. The self-centered chilliness of the English teacher deepened the solitary child's sense of isolation. Miss Grantley affected her like the embodied quintessence of censure upon all her moods and actions.

This lady always made Meg feel in the wrong. An increased brusqueness of gesture, a more rigid set of the defiant lips, expressed the protest of the wild little soul.

During the first week of her holidays she had a companion in her solitude. It was a battered doll, with rough hair and faded cheeks. It looked deserted. Rosamund Seely, a kind-hearted child, as a parting gift, had offered it to Meg on receiving the present of a beautiful new doll. "Poor Meg, you are going to be left alone. There's a dollie for you," the child had said, in transferring the belated toy; and Meg's desolate soul had been touched by the words.

For a week she had loyally carried the plaything about with her; she had perched it on a branch of the yew tree when she sat on her leafy throne; she had got to feel so lonely that she sometimes talked to it, and felt toward it as toward a companion, bidding her answer when she spoke. After awhile that constant comrade, sitting opposite to her with its grimy cheeks, its faded and ragged finery, became in its look of abandonment an emblem to Meg of herself. She grew to hate the sight of the doll; but still she would not part with it for the sake of the donor, and she thrust it in a corner of the shelf assigned to her in the dormitory.

The loneliness chilled the marrow of the child's life. The object ever in view, the repellent attitude toward her comrades, the consciousness that her replies were waited for and sometimes admired, had kept up Meg's spirit. It flagged in the length, the languor, the emptiness of those July days. There was nothing to be done but to sit up in the tree, to read, to think, and remember. As the hare seeks its form, so Meg's thoughts returned to the home where she had spent her childhood. She was always seeing that place on the stairs from which she had watched the coming and going of her only friend during those neglected years. Why did he not write to her? Why? Her lonely heart asked itself this question with insistence. He had promised to write to her, he was true, he never told a falsehood. Why did he not write? Then the conviction was borne in upon her that a letter was waiting for her at Mrs. Browne's house. Mr. Standish thought the landlady would forward it, but perhaps the stern white-haired gentleman, who told her she must forget her childhood and every one she had then met, would withhold her address from Mrs. Browne. The conviction haunted Meg. If she could but get to London she would make her way to Mrs. Browne and get that letter. Meg would lie awake, thinking of this, "If she could but get to London." The contemplation was still vague in her mind. It wanted something to condense it into a resolution, and that something came.

One late afternoon Meg sat at tea with Miss Grantley. She was always awkward under this lady's censorious glance. Stretching her hand for the bread and butter she upset her cup of milk on the teacher's dress. Miss Grantley had on her best mauve silk. She was going out to supper with a friend. As she wiped the stain from her draperies she looked icily at Meg.

"Your manners are deplorable, Miss Beecham. I do not wonder that your companions shun you. It must be most painful for young ladies to be associated with one who so richly deserves her nickname of the 'savage.'"

"I am not a savage," said Meg shortly.

"Do not answer me. Your untamed nature, which neither religion nor culture has softened, does not possess the very rudiments of civilized society. You shame this establishment. I had meant to take you out this evening."

"I would not have gone," retorted Meg, her eyes brilliant with indignation.

"Impudent little thing! Don't venture to talk to me like that!" and forgetting herself, Miss Grantley rose and gave a slap with the back of her hand on Meg's ear.

A fit of fury seized the child. She was once more the old wild Meg. She rushed into the garden, running blindly she knew not whither. A couple of slugs were crawling across her path. With an impulse of revenge she picked them up, and hurrying to Miss Grantley's room, hid them in the bonnet that lay on the bed ready to be put on.

From the dormitory Meg listened. She heard Miss Grantley go in, and when two short shrieks reached her ear she shook with impish laughter The next moment Miss Grantley appeared on the threshold.

"I know you did this," she said.

"I did," replied Meg.

"You might have given me my death. I might have had a fit. Miss Reeves comes home to-morrow, and the first thing I will do on her return is to report you to her. Meanwhile, you shall not leave this room."

Miss Grantley left, and Meg heard the key turn in the lock.

She was locked in.

A rush of passion swept over Meg as she realized that she was a captive. For a moment she stood stock still, thinking of all the terrible things Miss Grantley had said, realizing the bankruptcy of her little peace. She saw herself brought up solemnly before Miss Reeves, who appeared to her to live against a kind of ethereal background. A touch of fear chilled her courageous spirit. The silence of the school, the empty dormitory, deepened the impression of reprobation cast upon her. She felt herself disowned by a law-abiding community. Suddenly an idea came which held her breath in suspense—she would run away! She would go to London. There was a finger post on the highroad they sometimes passed in their walk which pointed to London. She would get out and follow that road, and make her way to Mrs. Browne. The immensity of the resolve overcame Meg for a moment. She walked restlessly up and down the room. Then, with shaking hands, she began to pack up her treasures. A spasm of excitement held her lips rigid as she set about collecting what she would take with her.

Goldsmith's "Animated Nature," the "Stories from the History of England," and "Cinderella," would go into one parcel with the little writing-case. She had still the brown paper and the bit of cord that had held them at her coming. The silver pencil-case and the roll of articles she resolved to carry inside the bodice of her dress. The single threepenny-piece with a hole through it which she possessed, a present from Mrs. Browne, she put into her pocket to serve in case of emergencies.

She would take nothing more with her.

As Meg was tying up her books she caught sight of the doll, with its demoralized, abandoned air, seeming to be watching her. With a movement of sudden, unaccountable anger she took it up and threw it to the furthest corner of the room.

Her preparations made, Meg began to turn over in her mind means of escape. She set about calculating the chances like a little general. She looked out of the window. The door being locked, this was her single means of exit. The porch stood right under the center dormitory window, the wall stretched sheer and blank between.

Meg was gazing down with neck craned to discover if the wall contained any chinks or irregularities that might serve as stepping-stones, when the door opened, and Rachel the housemaid entered, bringing Meg's supper on a tray.

Meg perceived that besides a liberal amount of bread and butter there was a large slice of currant cake.

Rachel was a conscientious and sullen young woman, who executed orders and delivered messages with the exactitude of a sundial and the surliness of a bulldog. She laid the tray sternly down.

"Cook sends her duty, miss, and this bit of cake which she made for the kitchen. She hopes you'll accept it."

"Thank cook kindly, and say I am much obliged," replied Meg with alacrity, recognizing the value of this contribution to her commissariat. The offering appeared to her in the light of a good omen.

Rachel received Meg's thanks in gruff silence, and departed, deliberately locking the door behind her.

Meg drank the tumbler of milk, but abstained from touching the provisions. She took a page of newspaper lining one of the drawers and carefully packed the cake and bread and butter, fastening this smaller parcel to the larger one of books.

Then again she returned to her meditations and calculations as to her mode of escape. If she had but a stout rope with which to swing herself down!

Then suddenly she remembered stories of hairbreadth escapes from fires, recounted to her by Mr. Standish, effected by the aid of a ladder made of sheets and blankets knotted together.

The materials were at hand with which to attain her freedom. Meg's mind was made up. As soon as she was safe from interruption: when Miss Grantley had returned and the household had retired to rest, she would begin making a ladder of sheets.

She determined not to go to bed, but to sit up till daybreak, and at the first streak of dawn scale the wall and escape.

Then she remembered that it would be probable that Miss Grantley would conform to the habit of the school, and make her round over the various rooms. At this thought Meg swiftly set about obliterating every trace of disorder from the dormitory. She stowed her parcel out of sight, and drew the curtains, and began to undress.

She was not yet in bed when she heard steps coming up the garden path and voices bidding each other good-night.

A few moments later the key of her door was turned, a step entered, and Meg heard the rustle of a silk dress. Miss Grantley was making her rounds. Meg appeared to be profoundly asleep; she was conscious of candle-light directed upon her face, but her eyelids did not quiver.

Miss Grantley stole out of the dormitory. Meg listened for the click of the key turned again upon her, but this time Miss Grantley contented herself with closing the door.

Meg could not believe her ears. She got out of bed, and by the moonlight she examined the lock. No, the second bolt was not drawn; the key was not turned. There was no necessity to make a ladder of bedclothes, no need to have recourse to this perilous mode of escape. This difficulty removed seemed like another good omen, an assurance of success to Meg.

She felt as if some guardian angel child were directing her project.

Before returning to bed, and when by the perfect silence she judged that all the household was asleep, she softly drew back the curtains from the windows. Then she lay down, determined to keep awake.

She would not go to sleep; she struggled to keep slumber at bay. She sat up when she felt drowsiness overtake her; unconsciously she slipped off into a doze. She had a dream, rather the sketch of a dream. She had a glimpse of a road—she was walking. She started up frightened, got out of bed, rubbed her eyes, plunged her face into water; she was wide awake now. Then she lay down again; unaware she dropped asleep.

CHAPTER XI.

AWAY.

The day had shot a golden arrow across the uncurtained window of the dormitory when Meg awoke. The sense of something to be done confusedly urged itself upon her mind, and she jumped out of bed. In a flash she remembered everything, and with trembling trepidation she asked herself was she late? Were the servants stirring? The profound silence in the house reassured her. Outside she saw the sky saffron and rose behind the trees, and she heard the birds singing their matins. Meg began to dress rapidly. She was careful in her speed. She was going on a long journey on foot, and she must not look like a little tramp.

Having completed her toilette she took up her parcel and softly opened the door. Her nerves were tense with excitement, and a restrained trembling shook her from head to foot. How still it was! She had a strange fancy; the silence seemed as though some unseen presence was there listening and watching. The shutters were closed everywhere; only a gleam of light flickered through the skylight on the lobby. If she stumbled she would wake some of the inmates; she kept thinking as she stole down. Once she nearly lost her footing. She fancied she had come to the last step of a flight of stairs when two or three still remained to descend. Had she not caught herself up in time she would have fallen, and, weighted as she was, the clatter would have been heard through the house.

As she crossed the hall she knocked up against something which fell with a muffled sound, that in the gulf of silence came like a boom. Meg listened. She heard the furtive clicking of a door above. She waited motionless. It was succeeded by no sound of footsteps, and she concluded it was the creaking of an unclosed door. Then she resumed her progress. She groped her way down to the kitchen—she knew there was no possibility of letting herself out by the hall door—it was dark there, and she knocked her foot against a chair and hurt herself. But she did not mind the pain. All her capabilities of feeling were strained in listening. Had she been heard? The silence still lay like a spell over the house. She shut the door that isolated the downstairs premises and she felt safer.

All depended still upon the caution of her movements, as she turned the key and unbarred the bolts of the door of the servants' exit. With determined quiet the deft brown hands proceeded upon their task when another danger met Meg. Pilot began to bark outside. His kennel was close to the kitchen door, and the furtive sounds had caught his ear and roused his suspicions. Every bark grew louder, and he growled savagely. Meg controlled the trembling that seized her, and the next movement opened the door and encountered the dog. Pilot was reputed dangerous by the schoolgirls, but Meg had no fear. In her isolation she had made friends with the mastiff. At sight of the little figure with hand uplifted to enjoin silence, Pilot paused in the spring he was crouching to make, and stopped barking.

"Hush, Pilot," whispered Meg in a concentrated voice; "don't bark, not on any account, Pilot! I am running away because I am miserable. Good-by, old Pilot!"

Pilot looked at Meg with questioning eyes, debating the reasonableness of her speech. He apparently hesitated to commend the step she was taking, for he did not return her greeting with any demonstration, but remained with head erect and pricked ears surveying her, and let her go in silence.

Meg went round to the kitchen-garden. She had decided to escape that way. The wall was covered with a trellis-work on which fruit was trained. Meg threw her parcel lightly over and began to clamber. She heard the unripe plums fall as she climbed with a sure-footedness that was one of her claims to the title of "savage" bestowed upon her by her schoolmates. With the agility of a squirrel she swung herself over and dropped among the nettles that grew at the base of the wall.

She sprang to her feet, picked up her parcel, conscious of one dominant emotion only—she was out of Moorhouse; she was free! Like a bird winging its way to more genial climes Meg dashed forward.

Across two fields at the back of the house, the bright road lay before her; her escape was made. Not a soul was up, and forgetting that she should economize her strength she ran gladly along, when suddenly an object arrested her eyes and riveted her to the spot. There, at the stile, facing the field, the path through which issued on to the highroad, stood a figure. The face was turned away, but Meg recognized that straight back, that dark dress with austere folds, that severe straw bonnet. It was Miss Grantley.

Was it some waking nightmare, an illusion of frightened fancy? Meg remembered the furtive click of the door. Could her escape have been discovered, and the mistress be lying in wait for her? With desperate resolve, after a moment, Meg determined to chance it. She would creep beside the hedge that led round the stile, and once on the other side she would trust to fortune and to her heels to escape pursuit. She began softly to move; a spray of woodbine caught her skirt—she disentangled it with trembling fingers; a puddle barred the way; she prepared to leap over it, watching that figure with terror. Something in its stillness, its stiffness, and its bent head frightened her. She thought she would call out and speak to it. As she hesitated the figure turned round, and Meg saw, not Miss Grantley, but a stranger whom she had seen at church and admired for her young and peaceful countenance. The lady was holding carefully something lying in her hollowed hand. Perceiving Meg she beckoned. The coil of fear about Meg's heart loosened, and she breathed again.

"Look at this poor chick!" said the stranger. "It has dropped from the nest. See how the mother is hovering round. Poor mother, we will not hurt your little one. God takes care of the fallen nestlings."

"Shall I put it back into the nest?" said Meg impulsively, feeling generous under the impression of that great relief.

"Can you climb?" said the stranger.

For answer Meg deposited her parcel and climbed up into the tree, then stretching out her hand she took the little bird tenderly, and in a moment she had softly dropped it back into the nest.

"That was a good action," said the lady, as she came down again, looking kindly at her. "I thought I was the only one out of doors—it is not yet five o'clock; but you have taken the conceit out of me. This is holiday time. Is that the way you take your holidays, by going out to walk at sunrise?"

Meg nodded. She was eager to dismiss the stranger; but still the lady dallied, looking kindly at her.

"There is a little nosegay; I picked it as I went out. I give it to you. Good-by!"

She took some flowers from her belt.

"Good-by," said Meg, with cordiality.

The stranger nodded again, and turning round walked away with swift and even steps.

Meg loitered a moment watching her, then she clambered over the stile and was off.

She sped along until she reached the highroad. She turned Londonward, not slackening her pace. Not a living soul was within sight or hearing. She had the road to herself. The sun was behind her. Her shadow stretched thin and long before her. It looked like her own ghost gliding in front of her and leading her on. Meg did not look about her, but she was conscious of a universal shining around her, of jocund shadows about her feet, of birds twittering, and delicate perfumes stirring through the breeze that blew so pure and fresh that it seemed to come from heaven's gate. She ran until she could run no more, then skirting the fields she walked quickly along. She thought it was another good omen that the day of her flight should be so brave and gladsome. Was nature rejoicing with her because she was hurrying to the place where she would hear news of the only friend she had in the world?

The hedges sparkled with dew; every bush and brake was hung with sheeny fragments of hoary silver that turned to gold in the sunlight. For her every blade of grass and little flower glistened with a limpid coronal. A thrush sang aloft in a tree; Meg thought it sang for her. After awhile she met a few laborers, but they took no notice of her. Their eyes were fixed on the ground.

As Meg walked along the assurance that a letter was awaiting her grew in intensity. She had heard that by steady walking London could be reached in six hours, seven at most. It was not five o'clock when she started. She would be in London by noon. She saw herself already entering the big city, asking her way to Queen Street; she would make straight for number 22 and ring the bell. Perhaps a strange servant would answer it; perhaps it would be Mrs. Browne herself. What a surprise, what exclamations, if it were the landlady who answered the door! But she would not reply to any questions until she had got her letter. "What letter?" "The letter that came for me with a foreign stamp," she would answer. "Ah, yes! it had come. How had she known it had come? There it was;" and she would take it to her attic, and sitting by the window she would read and read it till she knew every word of it by heart.

Meg passed a village. The people were astir in the streets, the shops were open. Everything sparkled in the sunshine and cast a blue shadow. A baby was crawling on all-fours, its little blue shadow by its side. A woman in the doorway with bare arms akimbo was chatting to a friend. Some geese were waddling down, moving spots of incomparable whiteness. A cart full of hay was standing in the glare of that morning sun. A red-armed girl was milking a patient cow, and there came the pleasant sound of the milk as it rushed into the pail. It was half-past eight by the church clock, the face of which was a blob of brightness. Miss Grantley and the servants had discovered her flight by this time. Perhaps they guessed that she was going toward London; perhaps that strange lady would tell! Meg at this thought left the road for the fields, and walked on the other side of the hedge. She tried to walk quicker to avoid pursuit; but all at once she began to feel as if she could not take another step. She was so tired. She was weak also from hunger. She must sit down and eat.

She had entered a meadow bordered at the further end by a stream. She crossed the grassy stretch, took off her shoes and stockings, and waded ankle-deep into the water. On the other side a little wood cast its shade. She would sit and take her pleasant rest there. The touch of the cool running water was delightful to her burning feet. She knelt on the opposite bank and bathed her hands and face. Then she sat down under a tree. It was delicious to rest; it was enough for a moment to feel how tired she was, to lean back and enjoy the support of that great trunk, and the shade of those leafy branches. No queen ever sat on a throne more restful, nor under a more dainty canopy. She took out the bread and butter—she would not touch the cake yet—and began to eat. She ate slowly. Her repast was a banquet. It tasted of all the penetrating sweet perfumes about her; of the honey-laden breeze, of the fruity sunshine.

When it was over Meg thought it would be pleasant to lie down and sleep. Then she rebuked herself. She had no time for sleep, she must get on to London. She had no time to waste; still she dallied. Nature had spread a couch of dried aromatic leaves for her, perfumed with sweet small flowers, guarded by a green barrier of bushes, shaded with a curtain of leaves. The soothing stillness of nature crooned to her a wordless lullaby. Meg stretched herself under the tree, drowsiness overcame her. She thought of the little bird that had fallen from its nest. Was she like that little bird which had dropped from its home of twigs? But she said to herself, "I put it back there."

Meg had a dream. The black slug had grown to an immense size, with its horns out. Its face seemed to grow like Miss Grantley's. Then it seemed to her that hostile inimical presences were around her, muttering. She woke; where was she? Who were around her? Brown eyes gazed down upon her from every side, warm breathings passed across her face, wide pink nostrils inquisitively moved up and down.

A forest of light-tipped horns surrounded her.

Meg started up. At the sudden movement the creatures jerked backward and took flight. She heard the clatter of hoofs; then pausing and huddling together, they turned and looked at her from a distance. Meg gazed back at them. She laughed; these woodland gossips were heifers—five heifers. She called to them, but they would not come. When she got up to approach them they scampered off.

CHAPTER XII.

AN ACQUAINTANCE BY THE WAY.

Meg decided that time for luncheon had come. The shadows lay long beside the trees and marked afternoon. She felt so rested as she blithely ate the piece of plum-cake saved from last night's supper that it seemed to her that she could walk all the way. It was a generous slice, and she threw crumbs for the birds, which flew down from the surrounding wood and became her guests.

Meg would have gladly dallied awhile, but time was pressing. She must get to London to-night. Taking off her shoes and stockings once more she crossed the stream, pausing a moment to enjoy the sense of the running water against her bare ankles. Then she determinedly resumed shoes and stockings, and after bathing her hands and face she turned to go on her way.

The road lay through hedges full of sweet-smelling eglantine and wild rose which stirred with every gust. As Meg trudged along she looked at the marks in the sand left by the feet which had come and gone across it that day. They made a confused pattern, through which here and there a footprint came out distinctly. There was one of a big nailed shoe that recurred with a sort of plodding regularity, and there was another of a dainty high-heeled boot that seemed to speed gayly along. There was a clumsy sprawling mark of a woman's foot that suggested slatternly shodding, and by its side that of a child's naked foot. Meg wondered if these were a mother and child, beggars going up to London. Presently another footmark attracted her attention. It was that of a single nailed boot, attended by what looked like the mark of one toe resting on the ground, surmounted by another mark. Together these two prints seemed to make a sign of admiration in the sand. Meg puzzled over this strange footmark till she forgot all the others. It fascinated her; preceding her like a cheery mystery. After a while the trace vanished. Meg watched for it; but it had gone, and with it the road seemed to her to have lost some of its interest. Presently she was startled by a "thump, thump" behind her. She felt a little startled, and she turned round to see who was coming. It was a lad swinging himself actively along on a high crutch. He soon overtook Meg, and as he passed he gave her a sidelong glance and touched his hat. He had a pleasant plain face, and bright brown eyes. She noticed that as he went along he left on the road that double mark that had such a quaint resemblance to a point of admiration.

Meg had returned his salute with a nod, which was not wanting in cordiality although it was somewhat stiff. This cripple seemed to her an acquaintance.

"Nice day, miss!" said the boy.

Meg nodded again.

"Going this way, miss?" continued the cripple.

"Yes," Meg replied, in a tone of embarrassed coolness, which was not, however, discouraging to conversation.

"Going far, miss?"

"Going to London," said Meg.

The cripple looked at her with evident admiration.

"Are you going to London?" asked Meg.

"No," replied the lad, "I'm going part of the way."

Meg did not like to press the question further, and the resources of conversation seemed exhausted.

"You see," said the boy after a pause, "I'm going to earn my livin' and the livin' of my mither and the little chap."

Meg looked at her companion with some surprise.

"I'm agoing to where I can earn thirteen pence a day; there's where I'm going. What I want is, they may want for nothink off there," and the boy, with a jerk of his chin, indicated a backward direction.

Meg felt curious to know how this crippled boy earned a living, but she did not like to inquire. So she said, with vague encouragement to further confidence, "You love them very much?"

"I love 'em," assented the cripple in a guarded tone. After a pause he continued, with more frankness, "I'm uncommon fond of the little chap. Mither can't earn enough, so he depends upon me, like. Now, how old do you think I am?" He straightened himself for her inspection, and leaned upon his crutch with the air of a soldier on parade.

Meg hesitated. The boy had a quaint, plucky face, childlike in line, and yet old by its expression of sagacity and caution. His arms and hands were well developed; one shriveled leg hung helpless at some distance from the ground. He seemed of no age and no distinct size.

"I cannot guess," said Meg. "I am eleven and a half," she added, with a generosity of confidence that invited a magnanimous return.

"I am fourteen come next March," said the boy. "Now you think I can't do nothink because of that ere leg." He glanced with some contempt down the maimed limb. "You thinks because I can't put my foot on the ground I can't do nothink. I can do everythink." The cripple turned with a swagger, and the children resumed their walk.

"I once punched a lad—he was older than me—who was worriting the little chap."

"You did?" said Meg admiringly.

"I did. He was striking the little chap in the face; and I comes upon him, and with my fist I gives him a blow, and before he can look up I hits him another, and when he knocks my crutch down I fastens upon him—I drags him down, that's what I does."

"You did right!" cried Meg.

"And I just gives it to him till he lies quiet as a lamb. And says I to him, 'If ye do it again I'll serves ye the likes again,' that what I says," concluded the cripple, marching along with a triumphant "thump, thump," of his crutch.

"I am glad you did it," said Meg, with a flush on her cheek and approval in her eye.

"That's what I does," repeated the cripple, with another swagger of his pendant body.

Meg began to feel a great respect for this cripple, who seemed to her to have the spirit of a lion.

"How are you going to earn money?" she asked, feeling an admiring friendship now justified the question.

The cripple, after a cautious moment, replied:

"Blacking boots."

"Oh!" said Meg, a little disconcerted.

"Faither was a dustman. I'd raither be a dustman than anythink. Ye've a cart, and there ye sits, and ye comes down only to clean away the rubbish; and sometimes ye find an elegant teaspoon, and ye may find a ring. Faither once found a gold ring with three red stones in it that shine. There's nothink like being a dustman," said the boy, with an air of one taking a survey of all the learned professions. "I'd be a dustman, but because of that ere leg. To be a dustman you must be hale in all yer limbs, ye must; so a lady comes round and says I'm to be a bootblack. She gives me brushes and a board and a pot of blacking, and I sets to; and I can make boots shine as will make your eyes blink. Now your boots," with a downward glance at Meg's feet, "are uncommon dusty—I'll black 'em for you."

Meg hesitated; but the cripple had already unstrapped the parcel swung on his back, taken from it a brush, a pot of blacking, and a board, and was down on one knee before her.

Meg could not refuse. She placed first one foot then the other on the board, and brush, brush went the active hands.

Meanwhile a big struggle was going on within Meg. She had no money but that threepenny-piece. Ought she to give it to the lad for blacking her boots? She put her hand into her pocket and turned the small silver piece about.

It was all that stood between her and penury. Still she could not accept a service without paying for it from this cripple, who was earning money for the "little chap."

"There!" said the boy rising, putting up his traps with an air of fine indifference to the effect produced by his action upon Meg's boots.

"I am very much obliged," said Meg hesitatingly; "and here is threepence."

"I don't want yer money," replied the boy with an emphatic jerk of his head. "Keep it; ye'll want it yerself."

Meg's admiration for her companion increased. She gazed down on her boots. "They're splendid," she said fervently; "I never thought boots could shine like that!"

"Well, I thinks as no one can beat me at blacking," said the cripple, accepting the compliment. "It's my notions as when the sloppy weather comes I'll make two shillings a day. But it's not a bootblack I'll remain."

"What will you become?" asked Meg.

"I do not mind telling you," replied the cripple with cautious slowness. "I'm going to be a joiner. Ye thinks as I can't. Ye thinks there's too much agin me. Why, everythink was agin me earning money. First that school-board, that was agin me. It wanted to set me all astray, spending time learning figures and spellin'; but I conquered the school-board. I gets too old for that after a bit. Then when I'm told by the lady of this situation in Weybridge to black boots every morning, there's fifty miles for me to get over; and here's the cripple boy agin, two miles from Weybridge!"

The lad gave a chuckle, a jerk of his head, and a thump of his crutch.

"You've walked fifty miles!" said Meg, with the homage of round-eyed surprise.

"Fifty miles," repeated the boy. "Then a friend o' mine is a carpenter. He would not trust me with a tool two years agone; and now I can plane and drive nails with the best of them. I had no money to buy a box of tools. I'm going to work for it with the boots. All I wants is the sloppy weather, and a spell of it, and that's enough for me."

Meg's admiration overflowed her pent-up heart, and moved her to confide in this cripple and ask his advice. She had not spoken to him of her schoolfellows, or of the object that had impelled her flight.

"Suppose," she began, "some one had been very kind to you, very good, would you not run away from people who were unkind to you, and laughed at you, and despised you?"

"No, I would stay to conquer them," said the cripple, stamping his crutch.

"How would you conquer them?" said Meg.

"I'd wear 'em out," said the lad. "Spite can't stand pluck; that's what I've found out. I'd give 'em a laugh, and if they pushed me hard I'd give 'em a slip of my crutch."

Meg was silent awhile with appreciation of such courage. Then she said:

"But suppose you felt sure there was a letter waiting for you, would you not go to get it?"

"Depends upon that ere letter," replied the cripple with circumspection. "If it was to tell me what to do to better myself I'd go and fetch it were it at the other end of the country."

"But," said Meg, with a quivering voice, letting out the secret fear at her heart, "suppose there was no letter waiting for you when you got to the place?"

"I'd go and look for the one as should ha' written it everywhere. I'd not give over till I found him," said the cripple.

"You would!" said Meg.

"I would!" repeated the boy.

"I wish you were going all the way to London," said Meg.

"To take care of you?" asked the lad. "Wish I could, but I can't, miss. I have the kid and the mistress to think of. It's not so far; to-morrow you'll get there."

"To-morrow!" repeated Meg, aghast.

"It's getting late," said the boy, "ye can't walk in the night. Now, what I say is, if ye find a barn, creep in there and lie in the straw; but if ye can get a hayrick and cover yerself all up to yer head, that's fit for a king—better than a bed. I've slept in 'em, so I ought to know."

Meg could not speak from consternation; the prospect for a moment overwhelmed her.

"Perhaps ye'll meet a cart, and the driver will give ye a lift. My faither once gave a lift in his cart to a little girl going toward London," the cripple suggested.

"I wish I could meet some one who would drive me," said Meg in faltering accents.

"If ye're frightened ye'll never find the person as was good to you," the lad replied rousingly.

"You were not frightened at night, all alone?" asked Meg.

"I'm frightened of nothink," said the lad; "but ye're a little lady, so that makes a difference."

Meg asked herself if her companion's shriveled leg did not make up for the disadvantages of sex, and she trudged along, resolved not to give in, but she wished she did not begin to feel so hungry again.

Presently they came to a fingerpost.

"What's written up there?" said the cripple.

"Can't you see?" asked Meg, astonished.

"I can't read," said the boy.

"Oh!" exclaimed Meg, whose admiration received a great shock.

"I'm ignorant," replied the boy, no whit disconcerted. "I'll conquer that, too. I conquered that school-board because I wanted to earn. I'll conquer ignorance; it's as bad as the school-board."

Meg's admiration revived.

"Weybridge is written on that side," she said.

"That's my way, then," said the cripple. "Good-by to ye, miss. I hope ye'll get all right. Don't forget the barn, or the hayrick if ye can get one."

"Good-by," said Meg, wishing to shake hands, yet hesitating.

The boy touched his hat and set off on his way.

CHAPTER XIII.

THE OLD GENTLEMAN AGAIN.

Meg listened to the thump, thump of the little crutch going off into the dusk, and to the sound of merry whistling, and she turned to pursue her way. The thought of that small lad with his crooked leg and his great courage roused her spirit. No obstacle now appeared too great to overcome, no road too long to walk in order to achieve her object; and she trudged bravely along.

She was very hungry. Her feet were beginning to ache again; but she was not going to stop yet; nothing would induce her to do this; so long as she could hold out she would walk. She would then look out for a proper resting-place in which to spend the night, and set off on her journey in the early morning. She tried to distract her mind by weighing the merits of sleeping up in a tree, or down on the ground, or in a haystack; but her thoughts would fix themselves upon nothing but upon something to eat and drink. She passed a village where all the cottagers seemed to be at their supper. Meg trudged valorously along, neither looking to right or left. Still she debated whether the time had come for breaking into that threepenny-piece. She looked at the matter all round. It stood between her and starvation. Until she reached Mrs. Browne's house she had nothing else to count upon.

Was she hungry enough yet? Had supper-time come? A whiff of the perfume of buns and hot loaves from a wayside shop decided the question. She felt weak and limp from longing for food, and she went in. There were tumblers of milk on the counter. A halfpennyworth of milk and a pennyworth of bread must make up her meal. The remaining penny and halfpenny must be left to pay for her breakfast to-morrow. She drank the milk in the shop, and she ate the bread in the open air, sitting on a common outside the village among great ferns. Meg thought she had never tasted bread so delicious as this. She felt as if she would like to sleep here among the crisp ferns; but she got up, resolved to walk all the way to London if the daylight would but last.

The fingerpost pointed down a road bordered on either side by pine trees. It ran through a wood. The west glowed before her, and the trees marshaled darkly against the light. The birds flew twittering across the sky, and all the insects seemed to be singing good-night to the day. The straight road seemed to stretch like a white ribbon before Meg. It was very lonely. She did not like the solitude; but she would not admit to herself that she was frightened. Yet an awe was creeping over her. The trees seemed supremely dignified. She felt very small and insignificant as she walked under their silence.

After awhile she heard a sound. It was a distant rumble. She looked round. A cart was coming along. It was filled with hay. Meg thought how pleasant it would be to creep within, tuck herself inside the hay, and sleep while the plodding horse bore her on to her destination. She loitered and waited until the cart passed, and then went right out into the road; but at the sight of the large, red-faced man, whose chin was resting on his chest and whose eyes were closed, Meg went quickly back into the path. The rumble of the cart died away, and again nothing was heard but the twitter of birds and the drone of the insects. Presently she heard a voice spreading in song through the dusk. It sang loud and discordantly. In Meg's childish experiences songs sung in such tones had a place; she gave a fierce little shiver, and hid behind the trees. She was naturally fearless; but she remained quiet as a little ghost until the figure, with unsteady gait, had passed. Then Meg resumed her way determinedly.

All at once she began to realize how tired she was. It seemed as if she had lost all her strength. She must lie down. In the faint light and silence, amid the calm trees, she must lie down and rest.

How quiet and still it was, as if all nature were bidding Meg trust to its protection and sleep till morning.

She looked around. There were no hayricks, but there were clumps of fern and soft sand covered thickly with the brown needles of pine. Then again Meg thought she heard the rumble of wheels, distant like wheels heard in a dream, not jolting wheels, but soft swift-rolling wheels. A carriage drawn by two horses was driving down the road toward London. Meg dreamily remembered how once she had driven in just such a beautiful carriage by Mr. Fullbloom's side; how easily they had traveled. In her weariness came a longing to be taken up into this carriage and to be driven along. She stood looking in its direction. It came nearer. It was an open carriage; a man was sitting inside it alone. She discerned the gleam of white hair on which the western light fell. Then she became aware of a stern face thrust forward, looking out at her. She had seen that face before. Where had she seen it? She dreamily remembered. It was that of the old gentleman who had bidden her never mention her childhood.

At a word from him the carriage stopped, and he beckoned to Meg. She hesitated to come forward; she felt inclined to run away. There was a vague motive in that impulse of flight. It partook of all the past alarm and misery, and she felt very much as if she stood on the brink of a precipice. The old gentleman beckoned again impatiently, and a grotesque idea flitted through Meg's mind that she must have lain under that tree, gone to sleep, and had a dream. The carriage, the horses, the servants, the dreaded old gentleman, were all a vision that would pass if she made an effort. She shut her eyes. When she opened them there was the figure still bending forward.

It beckoned to her. "Come here!" said a voice; but Meg did not move.

"Drive on!" exclaimed the impatient voice, and the carriage moved off.

A sudden revulsion of terror seized Meg as she watched it driving away. She roused herself and began to run.

Again the figure stooped forward—beckoned to her as the carriage stopped.

Meg approached.

"Are you not Meg—Meg Beecham?" the old gentleman said in a voice of stern surprise.

"Yes, sir," Meg answered faintly. There was a pause; the cold blue eyes rested heavily upon her as they had done that day, and their gaze suggested dislike.

"Come inside. I do not hear you," her interlocutor said, opening the carriage door. He did not stretch his hand out to help her; and Meg scrambled up, and at his bidding sat down on the seat opposite.

"Why are you here at this hour and alone? Why is your dress and your whole appearance so soiled and tattered? Have you strayed from your teachers? Have you lost your way?"

"No, sir," answered Meg.

"No, what?" repeated the old gentleman. "I do not understand your answer."

"I have not lost my way," said Meg.

"Then where are the persons in whose charge you are? Where are your schoolfellows?"

"They are not here. I did not go out with them," said Meg, and paused again.

Her dauntlessness was quelled by fatigue, and by the chill weight of these eyes fixed upon her.

"Will you answer me plainly? Why are you here, and why are you alone?"

"I have run away," said Meg with a flicker of her old spirit.

"Run away from school?" asked the old gentleman in an icy voice.

Meg nodded.

There was an awful pause.

"Why have you run away?"

"Because," said Meg, "they despise me—they say I shame the school. That's why I've run away."

"You say you have not lost your way," replied the old gentleman, taking no heed of her answer. "Where were you going to?"

"To London."

"To London!" repeated her interlocutor. "What would you have done there?"

"I would have gone to Mrs. Browne. I would have asked my way until I found her house."

There came a pause, during which the old gentleman looked at her and muttered himself.

Meg thought she heard him say, "Like parent, like child. The same evil disposition." Then lifting his voice, he called to the coachman, "Drive to Greyling; when you get there ask the way to Moorhouse, Miss Reeves' school for young ladies."

"No, no! I will not go back!—I will not!" cried Meg, jumping to her feet as the carriage began to turn round.

"You shall go back," said the old gentleman, pushing her down in the seat opposite and holding her there.

The carriage moved swiftly, and so noiselessly that Meg heard every word her companion said.

"You shall go back this time; but if ever you seek to run away from that school again, no one will take you back again. You shall be left to achieve your own willful ruin. I will wash my hands of you forever.

"Listen," he continued, with upraised finger, as Meg, awed by his manner, did not reply. "Do you know what will happen if you try to escape from that school again? You will become a pauper. You will have to beg by the roadside. You will sink lower and lower, until you get into the workhouse."

"No!" cried Meg, with a flash of confidence. "Mrs. Browne will take me in."

"Mrs. Browne has left that house. It is occupied by strangers who do not know you, who would shut its doors upon you."

"Gone!" repeated Meg, aghast. "Where is she gone to?"

"You will never know," said the stranger. Then after a moment he resumed: "If I had not been driving down that road this evening you would have begun your downward course already. Remember what I say to you. If you try to escape again you will become a little casual. A ruffianly porter will let you in and order you about, you will be put into a dirty bath, obliged to wear clothes other beggars have worn before you."

"No, no! It can't be—it won't be!" cried Meg.

"Who will prevent it?" said the old gentleman.

"Mr. Standish. He is my friend—he shall prevent it! I will write to him—he will fetch me away!" cried Meg incoherently, with a despairing sense of the futility of her assertions.

"Where will you write to him?" asked the stranger sharply. "Listen, child. You do not deserve that I should trouble myself on your account, and it seems as if you did not care to deserve that I should. There was one whom I loved who proved base and ungrateful. I left him to his fate."

He paused. Meg had not understood this mysterious speech. Her blood grew cold. After a moment the stranger resumed: "I do not doubt this Mr. Standish showed you much kindness, and I will not blame you because you are grateful to him; but from the moment you left your former life Mr. Standish passed out of it. He does not know where you are. He never will know. You do not know where he is. I do not know it; I could tell you nothing about him. Dismiss him from your thoughts." He made a gesture as if, with his uplifted hand, he were tearing the tie between her and that friend of her childhood. "Remember you owe duty and gratitude to another now. Be silent!"

"Oh, I want to know where he is—I want to know!" cried Meg, breaking again into incoherent appeal.

The old gentleman did not reply. He sat there silent, his face growing dimmer as the evening deepened. Suddenly Meg realized the desolation that had overtaken her, and throwing herself forward with her face prone down upon the cushions, she burst into weeping, with speechless sobs.

The stranger made no effort to comfort her. When the paroxysm of weeping had spent itself Meg turned her head, and saw that the night had come. The stars were out in the sky. By their light she dimly discerned the old gentleman's face. She thought that he was looking at her, then she saw that he lay back with his eyes closed, as if asleep.

She did not move. A hope and an assurance which had hitherto filled her heart had gone out of her life, and she lay there an atom of despair lost in a void of desolation. The carriage drove noiselessly on. She was vaguely aware of the still freshness of the night spreading about her. She knew when the carriage stopped, and when lights flashed, and familiar voices, speaking excitedly, sounded near. Still she did not stir.

She confusedly heard the old gentleman ask for Miss Reeves, and this lady reply. She recognized Miss Grantley's accents angrily asserting she ought not to be taken back. Then again she knew the stranger requested that she should be put to bed and given some food, while he had a private talk with the head-mistress.

Meg felt herself taken out; she recognized that she was in Rachel's arms. She was carried upstairs and undressed. She made no resistance, except to refuse the food Rachel pressed upon her.

At last she lay in bed and in the dark, communing and wrestling with her soul—living the troublous day over again. Sometimes thinking that she was once more struggling up that dusty highway; that she was falling and stumbling along; drifting away and then coming back to half-consciousness; and then dreamily hearing the thump, thump of crutches coming toward her, and catching a glimpse of a bright, bold face looking at her.

As she lay there oppressed by the weariness and bewilderment of that feverish time, a thirst for comfort rose in her little heart. She vaguely heard the rumble of carriage-wheels driving away, and she knew the old gentleman was gone.

In her sadness and longing for solace Meg was dropping off to sleep, when suddenly and softly she felt a kiss alight upon her forehead. She did not stir or question; she was too exhausted to wonder or to fear. After the day's fever and alarm she could not quail or wonder any more.

She fancied she heard light steps leave the room; but that kiss had brought the solace she yearned for, and she fell asleep.

CHAPTER XIV.

WHO GAVE THAT KISS.

A year and a half had elapsed since that wild outburst of rebellion against discipline had sent Meg flying Londonward. She had settled down into the routine of the school. Nothing now existed for her outside its boundaries. She had parted company with her childhood. The goblin past lay behind her, and as she looked back upon it the child who watched over the staircase almost appeared to have been a visionary creature.

She concentrated all her attention upon her studies. If still Miss Grantley was prejudiced against her she won the approbation of her other teachers. Signora Vallaria rolled her dark eyes as Meg's fingers still lagged behind in execution; but there was an energy, an intelligence in her apprehension that made the signora, while wringing her hands, yet consider Meg's lesson a treat to give. If Meg's answers occasionally still lacked exactitude in the historical class they were always roughly brilliant and intelligent. She was still apt to pass beyond her own depth, but her fellow-pupils felt the impetus of a rashness that was the outcome of energy. Meg had an unconscious ascendency over her schoolmates. A vigorous nature will always sway more languid spirits; but her influence over them was due rather to the fact that since she was eight years of age she had begun to think, and, like all suffering creatures, to observe. This power of observation, of drawing her own conclusions, and of acting upon them, was the secret of her ascendency over her schoolfellows. It was the ascendency of character.

Some called her repellent; for there was a childlike bluntness, a certain defiant awkwardness about her still. Others, like Miss Pinkett, treated her with contempt as a nameless waif. Others again, like Gwendoline Lister, wove a web of romance about her; nothing short of Meg being the deserted child of a duchess satisfied the Beauty. Meg knew she continued to be the object of this speculation, and these castles in the air made about her future wounded her, and she repelled curiosity. She still remained solitary in that busy republic of girls. Still her sensitive pride impelled her to refuse sweets when offered to her, because she had none to give in return; still she refused invitations, because she could not ask others to be guests at her home.

The day of her attempted flight had proved memorable; that day of feverish adventures had brought her an experience over which, in her loveless life, she often pondered. That spectral kiss placed on her forehead, which had brought such solace to her as she lay in misery and loneliness, haunted her. Who had given her that kiss? At first she had thought it might be Miss Reeves to assure her of pardon; but why should the schoolmistress have made a mystery of her kindness? The balanced composure and impartiality of the lady's manner dispelled this conjecture. The more Meg saw Miss Reeves the more she felt sure the lady would not yield to any emotional demonstration, and, if she yielded, she would not conceal it. Miss Grantley could not have taken this fit of pity. Her frosty behavior precluded its possibility. Then Meg thought it might be the cook who was kind to her.

"Did you come up to my room that night when I was going to sleep?" she asked the old servant; but the surprised denial she received was conclusive. Who then could have given her that kiss? It could not be the old gentleman. She had heard the wheels of his carriage driving down the garden, and nothing could well be more unlikely or unlike his stern, unsympathetic nature. There was no one else in the house that day except the servants, and no servant could have approached with that gliding footfall. Meg sometimes fancied it might be her dead mother attracted to her grieving child's bedside; but Meg asked herself, "If it were, why had she not come to kiss or comfort her before?" and then she added, "there are no such things as ghosts." But still this solution seemed to rest upon her mind as a notion more akin to her feelings, if it were the least probable explanation of the mystery.

Meg, during the year and a half that had elapsed, had given way to no more bursts of impish rage; she had become a reticent, grave, and silent girl. She was rather stern-looking, but this expression of sternness, if to a superficial observer it might have seemed an outcome of her nature, was in truth but that of a habit acquired by its enforced repression. Her sympathies bid fair to languish and die from want of soil, when an event happened which gave a force and a color to her school-life.

One afternoon after class, Meg, entering the schoolroom, perceived the girls gathered in a knot at the further end. She pushed her way through to discover what was attracting them. A golden-haired child was the center of the group. She was a new pupil come from India, and the girls were lavishing caresses upon the little stranger. The child was pretty and frail-looking enough to justify their enthusiastic effusiveness. She submitted to the kisses and hugs and general petting with a half-resigned air that suggested endurance of what she was already over-satiated with, rather than gratitude for the accorded welcome. Meg looked on, unsympathizing with these cheap caresses, but still attracted by the prettiness of the child as one might be by a strange bird of great beauty. The wistful gaze of large blue eyes encircled with lilac shadows met hers; but still Meg took no notice, repelled by that excess of demonstration lavished upon the little stranger by the other girls. "They don't see how they worry the poor little thing," she muttered as, taking up what she had come for, she went upstairs.

Some time after, as she knelt before her trunk, putting its contents in order, a slight touch on her elbow caused her to look round.

"What pretty things!" said a little voice. It was the child. With tiny fingers she pointed to the gayly-bound volume Meg was restoring to the box.

"There are pictures inside," Meg replied, turning the pages. The child looked coldly at the prints. She apparently did not care for the illustrations. It was the gold-edged leaves and the gold pattern on the cover which attracted her.

"How it *sines*!" she said with her baby lisp, and she passed her rosy fingertips over the gilding.

Meg looked at the bright hair falling in soft abundance over the tiny shoulders, at the dark lashes that shaded the eyes, surrounded by pearly shadows, at the sculptured lips, the upper lip lying softly curled over the lower. She thought she had never seen anything so dainty and delicate as this child. She seemed to be like a feather blown out of heaven across her path.

"What is your name?" asked Meg.

"Elsie," said the child; "and what is yours?"

"My name is Meg."

"Did your mamma give you those books?" asked the child.

"I have no mamma," Meg replied curtly.

"I have no mamma either; she is dead," said Elsie.

Meg was moved by one of those sudden emotions which come with a rush. She lifted her box with violence and carried it some paces off.

"How strong you are!" said the child. "Can you lift me?"

Meg felt inclined to be impatient. Then, meeting the glance of eyes the appeal of which was irresistible, she took the child in her arms and tossed her up.

That night, through the silence of the dormitory, Meg heard subdued sobbing. All the other girls were asleep. Elsie's bed had been placed on the other side of the room. Meg listened for a moment. Her heart was wrung by that low sound of weeping. She thought of her own anguish of loneliness, and of that haunting kiss which had brought such solace to her in her night of sorrow. After awhile she stole out of bed, and bending over the child, she kissed her forehead.

CHAPTER XV.

MISS PINKETT'S DIAMOND.

Elsie had taken a fancy to the stern, silent girl. She put out all her little arts to please Meg. Indifferent and inclined to be fitful to the girls who petted her and offered to carry her in their arms, she followed Meg about with pathetic persistence. Meg felt the delight of a devoted nature, thankful for opportunities given to it of sacrificing itself, and mingled gratitude with the feeling she returned. She devoted herself to Elsie. She played with her, she taught her lessons, she spent time and ingenuity in making learning easy to her; and Elsie accepted this devotion. There was pity for Elsie mingled in Meg's solicitude. She was so strong, and the child looked so frail. She was so fearless, and the child was as easily frightened as a little bird. A severe word made Elsie tremble; and it was pitiful to see the little hands, with their network of veins, trembling at any harshness.

The girls were astonished to see a return of the terrible Meg one day when Laura was teasing Elsie, mimicking her nervous ways, her frightened starts and turns of the head. Meg suddenly leaped forward and pushed Laura with such force that this damsel found herself sitting on the ground at some yards' distance.

"How dare you be so cruel to a little child!" Meg said, standing between Elsie and her tormentor.

"I shall have you punished, you gypsy!" Miss Laura replied.

"Have me punished if you like," said Meg; "but if you dare hurt this child I will give it to you again."

A peculiarity of the child which perplexed Meg, besides an almost abnormal timidity, was the singular fascination exercised over her by bright objects. Like a little grayling that rises to the light, every shining object attracted Elsie. It seemed almost uncanny to Meg, whose æsthetic sense was yet in its elementary stage, and who was unconsciously stirred by the moral suggestiveness of beauty, rather than by its physical appeal. Flowers, birds, Elsie herself, came to her as vague yet tangible revelations of a greater calm, a higher goodness and sweetness than earth holds. Elsie's delight in brilliancy was purely sensuous, and its influence over her nervous little frame puzzled Meg. A Salviati glass that stood in Miss Reeves' sanctum fascinated the child. She seized every opportunity to catch a sight of the wonderful vase; the shifting opal tints seemed to throw her into an excited dream. She would go and peep at it through the open door. Meg missed her one day from the playground, and found her perched on a chair in the room no one was allowed to enter without the mistress' permission, touching the vase, cooing and kissing the cold and glittering glass.

"Come down, Elsie! You must not come in here, you know, without Miss Reeves' permission," she said, alarmed, gently taking the child up in her arms. Then as Elsie struggled she went on: "Everything in this room is a present from an old pupil or a friend. Everything is very dear to Miss Reeves in it. She would be very angry if an accident happened to the vase. You would be punished for disobedience."

Elsie at this prospect let Meg carry her away, but she began to cry:

"I want it—I want it. I want to take it to bed with me! I want to have it all to myself!"

Meg soothed her. She endeavored to divert her attention by telling her the story of a mine of diamonds, more wonderful than that of the field of diamonds in "Sindbad the Sailor." For Elsie's sake Meg had developed the gift of telling stories. Her inventive powers were as the wand of a magician over the child. Her tales were distinguished by a touch of the grotesque and grewsome, a spice of humor and adventure. Meg's voice, which was of a peculiar quality, helped the effect. It was low and feeling at times, and again it had a spirited emphasis kept under gentle restraint. A child was the heroine of these stories, inspired by incidents enlarged upon and drawn from her childish recollections.

The stories that attracted Elsie most were those of splendor and of perfume. She would listen enthralled to the adventures in the bowels of the earth of a little girl, who met there the giant who took care of the fire, the sparks of which formed the diamonds, rubies, and topaz.

One day Elsie crept like a lizard to Meg's side. Miss Pinkett, who was a parlor-boarder now, had certain privileges, and was going to a party. She had called Elsie in to see her dressed, and she had shown the child a diamond star her father had sent from India on her last birthday.

"She put it here"—Elsie's little hand touched her forehead. "It looked all alive, twinkling—twinkling! It was more beautiful than the glass vase. It shot out now a lovely red ray, then a yellow light or a bit of shiny blue. Miss Pinkett said her mother had more beautiful diamonds," Elsie concluded, with a sigh of exhausted happiness.

"It is only a bit of coal—black coal that has been buried a long time in the earth," Meg replied with practical coldness.

"I don't believe it. It shines—shines—shines!" said the child. "Do you think Miss Pinkett would let me touch it, put it on, and play with it?"

"No," said Meg bluntly. "I would not ask her. You might lose it, and she would never forgive you."

But the diamond star had taken possession of Elsie's mind, and the fear of punishment did not lift the spell it exercised.

"Do you see that little red-morocco box?—it is in there. I saw her put it in there," she whispered to Meg next morning, dragging her by the skirt into the room Miss Pinkett still shared with Miss Lister alone.

"Do leave that diamond alone," said Meg brusquely. "Don't think of it so much, Elsie. It will get you into trouble and you will get punished. Did you ever see a drop of water through a microscope? That is ever so much more wonderful. Dr. Flite showed us this at the chemistry class this morning."

"I don't care for drops of water," said Elsie pettishly.

"There are monsters in it that fight each other and eat each other up. I'll tell you a story about a drop of water," said Meg suggestively, still trying to divert Elsie's attention.

One morning Meg was running down the corridor that led out of the dormitories.

"Meg, Meg!" called a little voice in a whisper. Meg looked round; it was Elsie standing at Miss Pinkett's door. She was holding something in the palm of her small, shaking hand. Meg, approaching, saw it was the diamond star.

"Elsie, put it back at once," she said peremptorily.

"The box was open. I saw it shining and I took it out. I could not help it. Is it not lovely?"

The tiny fingers caressed the stone, and the baby voice gurgled and laughed to it.

"You will get into trouble, and I shall not be able to save you from being punished," said Meg. "Put it back."

As she spoke Elsie gave a sudden start, dropped the diamond, and took to flight.

Meg picked up the gem and went inside the room to place it in its box. She encountered Miss Pinkett and Miss Lister coming in by another door.

"What are you doing in my room?" asked Miss Pinkett coldly.

Meg, without answering, put down the diamond.

Miss Pinkett flushed. "What right have you to touch anything of mine—this diamond especially?"

Meg remained silent, as if pondering what she would say.

"If I find you fingering anything that belongs to me I will report you, Miss Beecham," resumed Miss Pinkett in her most chilly tones.

"You ought to lock up your diamond," said Meg, at last, with an effort. "It it not right to leave it about—not right to others. It might bring some one into temptation."

"I understand," replied Miss Pinkett with cutting point. "I see there is necessity to lock it up." She shut the box with a snap, and closed the drawer with an elaborate jingle of keys.

The diamond was hidden, but Elsie still thought of it. One evening, as Meg sat on the window sill absorbed in reading an account of the condor, and following with tremendous interest the flight of the bird over mountain and seas, Elsie suddenly interrupted her.

She pointed to the evening star hanging in the suffused light of the sunset. "I wonder if papa sees that star in India," she said.

"Not just now, at any rate," answered Meg a little roughly. Any sign of yearning in Elsie's voice affected her painfully.

"Do you think Miss Pinkett's lovely jewel is like that star?" said Elsie, after a pause.

"No, it is not more like it than a lighted lucifer match is like a sun," replied Meg.

"She is gone out to a dinner-party to-night, and she did not wear it. I wonder why," continued the child, undismayed by the blunt reply.

"I do not care for that diamond more than if it were a pebble from the gravel of the playground," answered Meg impatiently; then with abrupt transition she asked, "Did you ever hear of the condor?"

"The what?" asked Elsie.

"The condor," repeated Meg, and she pointed to the picture of the bird. But Elsie's mind was not to be so easily diverted.

"If I had that diamond," she said in a subdued tone, "I would carry it about wherever I went. I would talk to it, and kiss it."

"I think," said Meg, "that if you had it you would want nothing but that hard, glittering stone."

"Nothing! At night I would put it under my pillow and it would come into a dream," continued Elsie.

"You dream of it already," said Meg impatiently.

"I wish you would tell me a story about it," replied Elsie with a sigh.

Meg shut her book. She drew her breath heavily

"I don't like that diamond," she said. Then pausing, she began abruptly:

"Once upon a time there was a little girl like you, who wanted a diamond, and she cared for nothing because she could not get that diamond; and a spirit put her into a small bare world all alone, to own it and be its queen. And the spirit gave her a beautiful diamond, twenty times as big and as beautiful as that one of Miss Pinkett's."

"Oh!" said Elsie, with a pant.

"The little girl," went on Meg, "jumped about for joy, and said she would want nothing now that she had this diamond.

"And the spirit said to her, 'There is something better and more beautiful than this diamond. When you have got tired of that jewel you will find this out, and then you will want that greater blessing.'"

"Blessing!" repeated Elsie petulantly. "I am sure she never did want anything more."

"And so the little girl," continued Meg, "talked to her diamond, and kissed it, and put it under her pillow at night and dreamed of it. But the diamond did not answer her, did not kiss her back; if she were sad or if she were glad it glittered the same. So the little girl at last grew tired of the diamond. It was not a companion. She felt a great want. There is something better, she thought; something that would be good and pleasant to have in sorrow as well as in joy. She asked the spirit to tell her what was that better thing. But the spirit did not answer. So the little girl went wandering about her bare world to find it. She walked till she was footsore, and still she could not find it; for she did not know what it was. Only she yearned for it. One night she was so weary and lonely that she felt as if she must die, and she prayed to the spirit to have pity upon her and give her that better thing; and at last it came to her."

"What was it?" said Elsie eagerly.

"She was dropping off to sleep, sobbing to herself in her weariness and solitariness, when on her forehead there was laid a soft kiss."

"A kiss!" repeated Elsie in a tone of disappointment.

"It was a kiss of love, like this," said Meg, bending forward and gently kissing Elsie's forehead. "And when she felt this kiss the fatigue, the loneliness and sadness left her, and the next morning she awoke quite happy."

"Was it the spirit gave her the kiss?" asked Elsie, with cold interest.

"She sometimes thought it was," said Meg.

"And the diamond—what became of the diamond?" asked Elsie.

"It had vanished," said Meg.

"I do not like that story," said Elsie pettishly; but she remained thoughtful by Meg's side.

CHAPTER XVI.

THE PARTY.

Meg thought that a change had come over Elsie. The child was attentive at her lessons, and softly dependent upon the protection of her friend. Elsie's mind had also become full of a school-party that was shortly to be given. There were to be theatricals. Miss Pinkett, who was to leave school after this term, was to play a grand piece on the pianoforte. The evening was to close with dancing. Some of the girls' brothers were asked to the party. Elsie was to take part in the theatricals—she was to appear as a fairy, in a white dress ornamented with tinsel.

Nothing else but the coming party was talked of. The girls discussed the festivity between lessons, and it was the theme of their speculation as they walked abroad. Meg alone was uninterested, and would have wished to escape and remain in her room that night. On the appointed day there were no lessons, and the schoolroom was decorated with flowers and sketches; the pupils lending their aid and their taste to Signora Vallaria, who supervised the arrangements.

The evening was approaching. All the girls who were to take part in the theatricals had dropped in one by one dressed for their parts. There was to be a rehearsal before the guests arrived. Elsie alone was missing. Meg sought her high and low. Once she thought she caught sight of the little figure in Miss Pinkett's room, but when she entered she found the room empty. As she was turning away she encountered Miss Pinkett, who looked at her with surprised coldness.

"I was looking for Elsie," Meg explained.

"She is not in the habit of coming into my room uninvited," replied Miss Pinkett. "Indeed no one is but yourself, Miss Beecham," and Miss Pinkett shut the door without waiting for Meg's reply.

The dress rehearsal had begun without Elsie, when suddenly the door flew open and Miss Pinkett entered in great agitation. Her diamond star was gone. Had any one seen it? The case was on the table where she had put it, but it was empty. Blank astonishment greeted the announcement. There was a rush to the young lady's room to help in the hunt for the missing jewel. The servants were called and asked if any of them had seen it; but all declared they had not entered that room. At last all adjourned to the schoolroom, where the wild excitement resolved itself into a solemn inquiry as to who had been last in Miss Pinkett's room. Whispers grew around Meg. More than one glance of suspicion was turned upon her. At last Miss Reeves asked quietly,

"What were you doing, Miss Beecham, in Miss Pinkett's room a little while ago?"

"I?" replied Meg, amazed.

"You cannot deny that you were there. I met you there!" Miss Pinkett rejoined excitedly.

"What do you mean?" said Meg. She looked round in a dazed manner, then a sudden fury gripped her throat as she understood the drift of the questions.

"Do you mean to say that you accuse me of stealing?"

"It does not amount to an accusation," said Miss Reeves. "I only ask you what you were doing in Miss Pinkett's room?"

"I never touched the diamond star," said Meg.

"Never! Do you mean," cried Miss Pinkett, "that you did not touch it that day I found you in my room with the diamond in your hand?"

"I touched it that day," said Meg, and paused; she had caught sight of Elsie, cowering pale and trembling against the wall.

"Why did you touch it? Why did you say I ought not to leave it about?" hotly questioned Miss Pinkett.

"I had a reason for touching it that day."

"What reason?" asked Miss Reeves.

"One which I cannot tell. It was a good reason. Believe it or not, I don't care. But I did not touch it to-day. I did not see it."

"You were in my room," said Miss Pinkett, "and the diamond case was on the table, and the diamond was in it, I know."

"I was in your room," Meg began.

"What for?" asked Miss Pinkett.

"I was looking"—again Meg encountered that appealing look from Elsie, cowering a white trembling little scrap against the wall.

"Your explanations are lame," said Miss Reeves gravely.

"I don't care if they are lame or not," Meg interrupted fiercely. "I have not taken that diamond. That is all I have to say. I have not taken it. I had it one day in my hand. Appearances may be so far against me; but if you condemn me on that, you do it out of your hatred to me."

"Hush, Miss Beecham!" said Miss Reeves severely.

"You hate and despise me because I have no one who belongs to me in the world," continued Meg. "You call me a gypsy girl and a tramp, that's what you call me. I don't care if you hate and despise me. I can't help what I was born, and I don't want to help it. What I know is that I have not taken that diamond."

A murmur ran round the room, but Meg did not pause to consider its nature. She turned in her ungovernable indignation, and pushing through her companions she flung open the door and slammed it after her. Again she caught a glimpse of Elsie's terrorized face and figure as she rushed past.

She went out into the playground to breathe the fresh air, trembling with fury. The old wild self had returned to her, taking with it seven devils. Her heart felt too big for her breast. Tearless sobs shook her as with all the vehemence of her spirit she repelled the charge brought against her.

Then again she seemed to see before her the wretched, cringing little figure of Elsie, and the large eyes fixed wistfully upon her. A suspicion fell cold and terrible on Meg's heart and checked her wrath. She had vaguely interpreted that look as an entreaty not to reveal Elsie's admiration for the gem. It seemed now to convey another meaning. How could she see that child alone, get a few secret words with her?

She went indoors, and in the hall she met Elsie, like a little ghost, furtively creeping out, holding something in her shaking hand.

"What is it, Elsie?"

"They are going to search our things, everybody's things," gasped Elsie. "I am going to throw it away."

"Throw what away?" asked Meg energetically.

"The diamond," the convulsive voice of the child answered; and still she held something tight hidden in the small shaking hand covered with a network of blue veins.

"Oh, Elsie, did you take the diamond?" asked Meg sadly.

"Yes, I thought—I thought Miss Pinkett would not wear it. I wanted to have it for one night. I—I thought she would not find it out. I heard her say she was not going to wear it. Where shall I throw it away?"

"You must not throw it away," said Meg. "Some one else would be suspected. Come, Elsie, you must be brave. You must say that you took it. Come with me, I'll say it for you."

She put her arm about the child. But Elsie struggled like a little mad animal from her grasp.

"No, no; don't say it was I—don't say it was I!"

An infinite compassion seized Meg when she saw the big tears welling in Elsie's eyes, and she asked herself how she could save this little one. Pity grew into the stronger motive and smothered fear. It was Meg's nature that what she undertook to do she did thoroughly.

"I will ask to be punished in your stead, Elsie," she said.

"They won't punish you for me—they won't let you be punished for me!"

Meg drew her breath.

"They don't think it is I—they don't think it is I!" sobbed Elsie, clinging to Meg. "Don't say it is I!"

The child was cold with anguish.

"Very well; I will not say it is you."

"You'll not say it—you'll not say it?" repeated Elsie, clinging to Meg's skirt.

"No; I'll manage it," said Meg.

"How will you manage it? Who will give the diamond up?"

"I," said Meg.

The child put her arms round Meg's neck, kissing her over and over again, and reiterating her cry not to say she had taken it.

Meg put her gently away, marched out and went straight into the room where all were assembled.

Miss Reeves with Signora Vallaria and two other teachers were preparing for the search of the boxes. Meg walked up to the head-mistress.

"There is the diamond!" she said, holding it out with outstretched hand.

A dead pause greeted this speech. Then Miss Pinkett's laugh rippled up.

"I thought so," she said.

Miss Reeves took the jewel, lifting her hand to enjoin silence.

"What does this mean?" she asked.

"I return Miss Pinkett's diamond," Meg replied.

"Do you mean to say that you took it notwithstanding your repudiation of the accusation which shamed some of us into believing you innocent?"

"I restore it now," said Meg huskily.

"Had you heard that the boxes were to be searched?" demanded Miss Reeves.

"Yes," said Meg.

Again there was a pause.

"I will stake my word upon it, there is a mystery," said Signora Vallaria, fixing her dark eyes upon Meg.

"Miss Beecham," resumed Miss Reeves, "did you take this diamond?"

Meg remained silent.

"I repeat the question," said Miss Reeves. "Did you take this diamond?"

"I restore it, and I am ready to submit to any punishment you may decree. Is that not sufficient answer?"

Again there was a murmur round the room.

"I am afraid it is a sufficient answer," said Miss Reeves gravely. "The punishment is expulsion from school. I give you till to-morrow morning, Miss Beecham, to explain your strange conduct. You cannot attend the party. You have turned an occasion of festivity into one of humiliation and unhappiness for us all. Go upstairs. You can no longer occupy the dormitory with your fellow-pupils. You will be taken to a room on the other side of the corridor where you will sleep alone. Miss Grantley will show you the way."

Meg turned to follow her guide in silence. The stern girl seemed turned to stone.

CHAPTER XVII.

POOR MEG.

Through the evening Meg heard the intolerable dance music going on and on. Little by little there came to her in her isolation the realization of the thankless load she had taken upon herself—a burden of guilt of the meanest kind. What would Mr. Standish think of her now? He had for some time past fallen into the background of her thoughts; but now there returned to her the memory of this friend of her childhood. With anguish she felt that when they met again, instead of appearing before him grown into a lady, full of the grace of blossomed womanly ways, and with the dignity which comes of loving protection to the weak, what would she seem to him? For years, thought Meg, for all her life, she must seem a miserable wretch and a thief.

She walked up and down the little room contemplating this picture. She could not face the prospect; and still, as there rose before her that vision of a cringing, shrinking child, an atom of terror outlined there against the darkness, appealing to her, Meg once more took up the load of guilt. Up and down she wandered, unable to concentrate her thoughts, sometimes contemplating how two hours ago she was a different being—all the change that had happened in two little hours!—then feeling that one comfort remained to her—the thought of Elsie's gratitude. In an alien world this little blossom of love would sweeten her lot. She turned from the realization of her own ruin to linger on this consolation that round Elsie's heart would hang the rich perfume of thankfulness for the sacrifice she had made. And then still, as she walked up and down, she thought how downstairs as they danced they all knew it. She was worse to them than a beggar in the streets. "If I were to go downstairs they would all shrink from me," she muttered bitterly. There was a stain upon her never to be wiped off. In two years would it be forgotten? she asked herself drearily. No, it would not. In three years? No, it never will, answered the thought; and then always, like the burden of her plaint, that Mr. Standish would hear of it.

The intolerable dance music stopped at last. She heard the rustle of dresses, the rush of feet. The party was over. The girls were going to bed. The gas was turned off and the house was plunged into darkness.

Meg lay down upon her bed and from sheer fatigue of sorrow fell asleep. She woke with the dawn, and for a moment she forgot what had happened. Then the heavy misery shaped itself and pressed upon her soul again. The calm morning held a promise of hope. What would the day bring her? Would not Elsie tell?

Just before the bell for prayers rang she heard a step outside. The handle of the door turned and Miss Reeves entered.

There was a moment of silence as the head mistress and the pupil faced each other.

"Meg, how did that diamond come into your possession?" Miss Reeves asked, not unkindly.

Meg did not answer.

"Will you not explain? I have come here to win your confidence. Why did you not return it before the order came for searching the boxes?"

A passing moment of temptation came to Meg to explain, to admit that certain reasons kept her silent, but she sternly repressed the impulse.

She repeated what she had said before—she had restored the jewel, was that not enough? She would say nothing more.

"Then," said Miss Reeves sternly, "I can give but one interpretation to your obstinate silence. You are guilty of an act which seems to me the meanest that ever occurred in my school. There remains but one course for me to take. I will write to your guardian. You must be removed at once. The disgrace of your presence must be removed from your comrades. You will join your schoolfellows at prayer-times only. Your meals will be brought up and served to you here. I must forbid you to address any of your schoolfellows; nor must you speak to any of your teachers except to make the small reparation of a full confession."

Miss Reeves turned and left the room with cold stateliness. Meg remained standing where she was till the prayer-bell rang. The fury of the night was over. Her mind seemed a void. She could think no more, scarcely could she suffer. When the bell ceased, she left the room. A few laggard girls were hurrying out of the dormitory. They passed her with averted faces and in silence; and they whispered with each other. There came upon Meg the first bitterness of the realization that she was an outcast from the community.

She entered the room where all were assembled, feeling dizzy. Then a sort of courage of indignation came upon her, for she was innocent. She looked in the direction of Elsie's place, eager to receive a glance that would repay her for all that she was bearing; but Elsie's eyes were carefully turned in another direction, and she appeared bent upon hiding behind another girl, as if to avoid seeing Meg. A pang of anguish shot through Meg's heart. Was that little hand lifted with the others against her? Was Elsie also thrusting her out as did all those who refused her fellowship in their lot? She felt so dazed that she remained for a moment standing, unaware of the general kneeling around her as Miss Reeves' voice was raised in prayer. Then her heart began to harden, and she looked toward Elsie no more.

When the girls were filing out she thought she would give Elsie another chance. The child must pass her in going out. Meg was conscious of her pet's approach, although she did not openly look her way. She felt if she watched Elsie and the child made an advance it would not be spontaneous. And yet, when there came no furtive touch on her hand, no whispered word as Elsie passed, Meg could not withhold from glancing toward her. Yes, Elsie had passed with eyes averted. That last link of sympathy which had given her hope gave way and broke.

Meg went up to her room, and the day passed. She sat with her chin buried in her hands looking heavily out. She felt stunned; she no longer protested or pondered over the future. At prayer-time that evening she did not look toward Elsie.

The next morning there was again a moment of forgetfulness when she awoke. Then again the horror gradually shaped itself, but this morning nature brought to her no reassurance. At the sound of the bell Meg rose with a heart like lead. She dressed herself and went down slowly. A mood of indignant bitterness had replaced the chilled misery of her bewildered heart. After prayers Miss Reeves informed her that she had received a letter from Mr. Fullbloom. He would fetch her away that afternoon. She must be prepared to leave then.

Meg received the news mutely, and went upstairs to begin her packing as directed.

She mechanically folded and put her belongings into her trunk. When she took out the presents Mr. Standish had given her, and that bore the marks of much handling, a movement of enraged despair seized her, and she trembled. "He'll never care to see me again, and how could I see him?" she muttered.

The girls were out in the playground as she finished her task. "I'll be glad to get away!" she said, as she sat on her box a moment and looked round her. But even as she said this her mind called up before her the departure. "Where am I going to?" she muttered. With compressed lips she whispered to herself as she rose, "No matter! no matter!"

It was two o'clock; in less than an hour she knew Mr. Fullbloom would be here. Her trunk, locked and strapped, stood in a corner; her hat and cloak lay upon it ready to be put on at his summons. No one had come near her. All her preparations were made. The old restlessness had returned; and she was walking up and down, thinking, thinking where was she to go to. What would happen to her?

"Meg! Meg!" said a little voice in a whisper. She turned; it was Elsie standing on the threshold of the door. There was a pause, during which Meg eyed the little figure, huddling up into a corner, its hands convulsively working together with a pitiful resemblance to older grief.

"Speak to me, Meg! won't you speak to me? I am so miserable," lisped the child piteously.

"You ought to be," replied Meg.

"If they would only let me go away with you!" moaned the child. "Oh, Meg, if they would only let me go away with you!"

"How could they let you go with me? I am a thief; you are a white, pure, innocent child," Meg said in bitter sarcasm.

"It is I who am wicked, not you. Oh, Meg, I love you so much, I love you so much!" reiterated the child, with that piteous quaver in her voice, stealing into the room, still wringing her little hands.

"Love me!" repeated Meg, her voice shrilly bitter; "and you do as the others do. You turn your face away when I come into the room."

"I am frightened, I am frightened. The girls say no one must look at you, or talk to you. I am frightened."

"Yes, I know you are frightened," Meg replied with softened gruffness. Elsie looked changed, she seemed a little wasted.

"I cannot sleep. Oh, Meg, I cannot sleep, I am so miserable!" sobbed Elsie, touching Meg's dress.

A pang of pity shot through Meg's heart.

"Hush! Elsie. Never mind, never mind," she said, stroking the child's hair. "Don't speak loud, some one may be listening."

"I wish I could tell," said Elsie, with heaving bosom. "I try to make myself tell. It stops here!" and the child put her hand to her throat. "I try to say I took it; but I can't, I can't. And you won't tell, Meg, you won't tell?"

"No, I won't," said Meg. "I won't. Do not be afraid, my pet."

She kept stroking Elsie's hair, grateful for that moment of solace.

"I wish I were dead!" cried Elsie, with a sudden wail, flinging herself into Meg's arms.

"Come away this moment!" said a voice, and a hand took hold of Elsie and dragged her away.

Meg recognized Ursula. She stood stock-still for a moment. Then she threw herself prone down upon the ground with a passionate cry.

That touch of comfort so rudely taken from her; that word of love from the child who had most right to give her love, silenced so abruptly! Why? Because in their rude honesty her comrades had decreed to exile her and abhor her like a thief.

She remained with her face pressed down to the ground, as if she would press herself into the heart of the cold floor. Vaguely she was aware of the bell ringing as for classes, and she knew the time had come—in a few moments more she would be gone on her way. But she did not move.

She became aware of steps approaching. Some one touched her on the shoulder. Ursula's voice said, "Meg, you must come down at once."

Meg turned her head round.

"You must come down at once," repeated Ursula, as Meg kept looking at her stupidly. "You had better come down," continued Ursula gently, putting her hand upon hers. Meg rose.

"I am going, but I will go alone," she said with returning fierceness, flinging Ursula's hand away. She pushed her hair roughly from her eyes and went toward her trunk to put on her hat and cloak.

"You need not put on your things," said Ursula. "It is in the schoolroom you are wanted."

"In the schoolroom? Very well," said Meg. She passed Ursula. She went downstairs, and with a reckless bang she opened the schoolroom door. What new ordeal or humiliation was awaiting her?

The room was full. Miss Reeves advanced to meet her.

"Miss Beecham," said the head-mistress, "Elsie has confessed everything. Young ladies, I have sent for you all, for before you all Miss Beecham was declared guilty and before you all she must be cleared of this charge. She is entirely innocent."

The ground seemed to sink under Meg's feet; the surroundings to fade away as in a splendor. She was aware of a murmur all round her, of the girls looking at her with a new expression of regret.

"Has Elsie confessed?" she panted.

"Not of her own free will," replied Miss Reeves gravely. "She was forced to confess by the suddenness of Ursula's action. Ursula had crept up to say good-by to you. She never thought you guilty. When she came into your room she overheard enough to convince her of the truth. She dragged Elsie before me, and forced her to tell. It was not a right thing, Meg, to shield this action. But it was so generous I cannot blame you. You were ready to sacrifice yourself for a child who would have let you go forth disgraced."

"It was splendid!" said Ursula. "Meg Beecham is a noble girl."

"She is," circled round the room.

Then Miss Pinkett stepped forth, elegant and straight-backed even in her evident emotion. Tears stood in her eyes, yet her voice was high-pitched and smooth.

"I beg your pardon, Miss Beecham; I apologize with all my heart to you. It was I who first accused you. Will you forgive me?"

"I forgive you," said Meg automatically, taking Miss Pinkett's extended hand. Then Ursula, with spectacles shining with tears, came forward and kissed Meg, who received the embrace in the same dazed fashion. All the girls trooped around, taking her listless hand.

Suddenly Meg recognized Elsie standing alone, wringing her little hands with that piteous gesture of older grieving. Sinking down on her knees, she stretched out her arms.

"Elsie, Elsie!" she cried, and in a moment the sobbing child was clasped to her heart.

"Oh, Miss Reeves, Miss Pinkett, young ladies!" said Meg, looking round, holding Elsie tight, tears coursing down her cheeks, "do not punish her, she is so little, so tender. She took the diamond as a child might take a shining bit of glass, only because it was pretty. Do not punish her, she is so delicate, so little! It was fright that kept her silent. Forgive her!"

There was a pause, broken by Elsie's sobs, repeated in various corners of the room.

"How can Elsie be forgiven?" said Miss Reeves gravely. "Worse than taking the diamond was her willingness to let another be expelled."

Then again Miss Pinkett stepped forward.

"Madam," she said, "we owe Meg Beecham some reparation. I owe it to her more than any one. For Meg's sake, pray let Elsie go unpunished!"

"For Meg's sake!" said Ursula, seconding Miss Pinkett's petition.

"For Meg's sake!" was repeated all round the room.

Miss Reeves hesitated. Then laying her hand on Elsie's head:

"Let it be so. For Meg's sake you shall be forgiven; for the sake of the girl whom you would have injured beyond words to tell, you shall go unpunished. This miserable incident will never be referred to again. That is all that we can do to make it up to Meg—to forgive you, Elsie, for her sake."

CHAPTER XVIII.

PEACE.

Meg was courted now by her schoolfellows; but the attention lavished upon her wounded her pride. She measured by it the contempt that had so easily accused her of thieving. To her sensitive spirit this kindness seemed insulting. It said, "We thought you a thief, and we find you are not." She responded coldly to advances made to her by all but Ursula.

The girls did not reproach Elsie; a sense of fair play kept them from referring to the diamond episode, but they shunned her. They stuck to the letter of the promised forgiveness, but they did not forget that she was a little thief. Meg watched the small figure lying apart and solitary in the play-hours—a white drift upon the bench.

Her heart bled. The child had been so caressed before, and was now an outcast. She remembered how she, too, had been neglected and shunned; but she was strong, and had never known petting, and her anger was stirred against the girls.

She tried to make it up to Elsie; but a change had come over the child, and she shrank from her friend. Meg knew Elsie felt ashamed, and she busied herself about the child to prove that the sorrowful time was not forgiven only, but forgotten also. She watched her opportunities to help the little one at her lessons; to put away her books, pencils, and other belongings. Elsie refused help, and avoided giving Meg those opportunities. The old clinging ways were gone. The chattering voice was hushed. A circle of ice seemed to surround the child.

Meg felt lonely and blank; and pity mingled with her desolateness. All the graceful radiance of childhood had gone from Elsie. Meg knew the change was due to remorse; the shyness of guilt was upon Elsie's heart. She longed to make the child smile and prattle again. As Elsie had longed for that foolish diamond, so Meg longed for Elsie's smile and prattle.

April had come; there were violets and primroses in the woods about Moorhouse, and Miss Reeves announced that the Saturday half-holiday might be spent afield. Meg determined that to-day she would conquer her pet's shrinking—that she would win that laugh. She went to look for Elsie. She found her lying listlessly on a bench in the sunshine. As she approached Elsie turned her face away.

"We are going out into the country to pick flowers," said Meg, kneeling beside her.

Elsie did not answer, and made a little movement with her elbow as if to wave Meg away.

"We are not to walk two and two together like soldiers," Meg went on, taking no notice. "When we get to the woods we are to break up our ranks and run wild. You and I will hunt for violets together."

"I don't want to go," said Elsie.

"You are not well, my pet," said Meg, patting the little hand.

"I am quite well," said Elsie harshly. "I do not want to go, that is all."

"Then I will not go either. I will stop with you," said Meg determinedly.

"No, no, no. I don't want you to stop with me! I don't want you!" replied Elsie with hurried emphasis. "I want to be alone. Of all the girls you are the one I want most to be left alone by."

"Why do you hate me, Elsie?" asked Meg gently.

"I don't hate you," replied Elsie, after a pause, in a faint, quavering voice. Then she added with labored utterance: "I am ashamed. Every time you look at me, every time you come near me, I am ashamed." Her voice gathered energy, while her breast heaved with tearless sobs. "The other girls look at me as if they were always thinking 'She is a thief,' and I don't mind—their looks not half (sob, sob) so much—as—I mind—your kind look. It makes me think—of—my dreadful wickedness."

"I look at you like that because I love you so dearly," said Meg, seeking to draw the child to her.

Elsie struggled and sobbed, but at last she let Meg take her on her lap and lean her cheek down on her head. It seemed to Meg as if the circle of ice were broken. She did not know what to say that would soothe that stricken little conscience, and yet guide it. All she could do was to hold the sobbing child tight.

It was one of those beautiful days in spring when everything seems careless and fond. The trees rustled around them as if hushing the voice of sorrow. The flowers looked up with bright faces; the indulgent sunshine shed its broad light. Everything seemed so much in contrast with the grieving child that Meg could think of nothing but to set herself to make that little pale face smile again. The child used in her happier moments to be fond of playing a game of shop. Meg excelled in mimicking the various customers coming to buy. Taking her ribbon now from her throat she set it up for sale, and became in turns the querulous customer, the fat fussy customer, the French customer. As she gesticulated, shaking her fingers up in the air, shrugging her shoulders, and talking in French, bargaining, vowing it was *trop cher*, she acted her part so vividly that Elsie forgot her sorrow, and at last broke out into a laugh.

From that day Elsie clung to Meg. The girls continued to abstain from referring to the incident of the diamond, and Miss Pinkett was elaborately kind; but Elsie was reminded of her sin by the emphasis of absolution around her. She still shrank from the companionship of other girls. With Meg alone she was forgetful of the past. The tie between them was recognized, and during the constitutional walks of the schoolgirls Elsie was allowed to leave her place among the younger ones and walk with her friend. These walks now lay toward the country, away from the village, where an outbreak of scarlatina was raging. In the blue-rimmed land, with its misty embattlement of downs outlined against the sky, through the shade and flicker of woods, through lanes sweet with the bravery of floral walls, the girls walked; and to Elsie Meg became the mouthpiece of nature. Those walks in the countryside were at this time the happy hours of Meg's life. The sensitive little hand in hers, that responded so quickly to her own delight, helped the inspiration that came to her from the illusive cloudland overhead, from wooded aisles, spread with wild flowers, voiced with notes of birds and buzz of insects.

This part of Meg's school-life came to an abrupt conclusion. One morning Elsie did not come down to breakfast. That evening she had a little fever, and the child's throat was sore. The doctor came, and the word "scarlatina" was whispered. In a few days the school was empty of the girls. Meg alone remained as usual. Every precaution to prevent infection was taken by Miss Reeves, and Elsie was isolated.

A new anxiety now sprang up in Meg's heart. Her thoughts were ever in the room at the top of the house, with the heavy curtains drawn before the door, from which distilled an acrid smell of disinfectants. Often Meg crept upstairs and listened. She watched every day for the doctor, to ask how Elsie was. The answers were always vague. In a few days the crisis would come. There was a tantalizing mystery in these replies, always followed by the injunction not to go near the child.

"Does she ever ask for me?" asked Meg.

"She is delirious, she would not know you," was the invariable answer.

One morning the news came that the crisis was past—delirium was over. The news was good; yet the doctor's face looked grave. Meg overheard him say to Miss Reeves that Elsie might sink from weakness. The child's feebleness baffled him.

"When shall I see her?" asked Meg huskily.

"Not just yet," the doctor replied, patting her head.

That night a storm of wind raged outside. Meg listened to the howl of the wind, to the lashing of the trees bending their backs to the scourge. The doors creaked; Pilot was dragging at his chain. Meg's thoughts were with Elsie. The contrast of her feebleness and the force raging outside seemed to haunt her. She fell asleep, and she dreamed that Elsie was dead. She saw her distinctly, a white, piteous figure lying very still, beaten down by some pitiless assailant who had left her there. Meg awoke with a start. The storm was over, but Elsie had called her.

"Meg, Meg, come!"

Was that cry part of her dream? She sat up rigid, her ears strained, every nerve on the alert, listening. Through the silence the call came again:

"Meg, Meg, come!"

She could not have told if she heard it with her physical ears. Elsie wanted her; that was all she knew. She was out of bed in a moment. A determination strong as had been that former idea of flight impelled her. She would see her pet. If she caught the infection and died, what mattered it? She would go to Elsie, the child wanted her.

A pale light flickered through the space of windows left uncovered by the shutters. Meg made her way cautiously, yet swiftly. It seemed to her that Elsie knew she was coming, and that there was no time to be lost. A jet of gas was burning low in the passage at the end of which was the curtained door. Meg lifted the heavy drapery. The scent of the carbolic grew more acrid. She pushed her head through the door that stood slightly ajar. The nurse, lying on a couch, was asleep. Meg at first could not see Elsie, but when she made a few steps inside the room she perceived the child.

Elsie's eyes were turned toward the door, as if anxiously watching. As Meg entered she made a little ghostly gesture, as if trying to get up. Meg was by her bedside in a moment. She had an impression that it was Elsie and yet not Elsie who was there. The beautiful hair was all cut off. The face was shrunk, a distressed expression rumpled the brow. The eyes were very bright and wide open. They seemed to Meg Elsie's eyes looking at her from a distance. As she clasped the child in her arms she realized with despair that it was like clasping a small gasping phantom.

"I thought you would never come, Meg," Elsie murmured through her labored breathing.

"Oh, Elsie, I have wanted to come," whispered Meg, bringing her face close down to the pillow.

"I wanted you," whispered Elsie. "I kept saying, 'Meg, Meg, come!'"

"I heard you," said Meg.

"Heard me?" repeated the muffled voice. "How could you hear me? I only whispered it. 'Meg Meg, come!'"

"But I heard you," said Meg, "and here I am, darling; here I am, and I will never leave you."

"I said," continued Elsie in that labored whisper, "if Meg comes the dreadful diamond will go."

"The dreadful diamond?" repeated Meg.

"It was always there; and sometimes it grew big, big, like a shining mountain, and put itself here." The spectral hand placed itself on the tiny chest. "It was heavy and cold—it pressed me down."

"It was a bad dream, my pet; not reality," said Meg soothingly.

"I saw it always, shining red, blue, and green. It shone in the dark as in the light, and sometimes it was like a great bright eye looking at me—always looking at me. It moved when I moved, and seemed to say, 'You nearly had Meg turned away like a thief.'"

"No, no; it was not you, it was I—I who did it all of my own free will," cried Meg, kissing the cold face that had become the emblem round which gathered her tenderest emotions.

"But it won't come again, because you have kissed me. The kiss that is better than the diamond," said Elsie with a vague relief in her panting voice.

"It will never come again," repeated Meg, trying to still her sobs.

Elsie lay back apparently at peace. Suddenly she turned, and there was a flicker of the old trouble in her eyes.

"Do you think God, too, forgives me?"

"Yes," replied Meg with a bursting heart.

"Are you sure he does?" insisted the piteous, laboring voice.

"I am sure of it, I know it!" said Meg with a world of conviction.

Elsie sighed, closed her eyes, and there was a silence. Meg thought she was asleep, when she opened her eyes again and looked round with a troubled movement.

"It is very dark," she said. "Draw back the curtains and let in the light."

"It is not day yet," said Meg.

"Stay with me, it is so dark," gasped Elsie, her hands restlessly moving as if pushing back some weight.

"I will not stir from your side, my pet," said Meg, stilling her sobs.

The gray light was stealing in. The tired nurse still slept. Meg saw the remote expression in the sick child's eyes growing more remote.

Suddenly Elsie made another ghostly attempt to sit up.

"How sweet the lilac smells!" she said. "Here is London-pride, and there's thrift. I'll pluck these for Mamey."

She struggled to get out of bed, while Meg held her tight.

"Mamey calls to me—to—say—good-night—and say my prayers," she panted, and then dropped back.

The blue lips moved as if speaking; but Meg could not distinguish the words. A realization that the child was slipping away, that phantoms were about her as she stood on the threshold of the other world, came upon Meg with an anguish of awe.

"Our Father," she began softly, impelled to pray; but Elsie seemed to pay no heed. The little hands still stirred uneasily. The lips still moved. At last Meg distinguished some broken words: "Forgive us our trespasses—as—as—Meg forgives." There came a sigh, the lips stopped muttering, and only the waxen image of what had been Elsie lay on the bed.

––––––––––––––––

CHAPTER XIX.

WHO IS HE?

Five years had elapsed. Meg was eighteen; she had distanced all her competitors, and she was the head-pupil of Miss Reeves' establishment.

During those years she still remained somewhat of a solitary in the school. The girls who had been her first schoolfellows had all left. By the succeeding girls, Meg was still called repellent by some, attractive by others.

As time went on the mystery of her origin, about which her schoolmates still busied themselves, pained and humiliated her with greater poignancy. She longed to be allowed to know and love her benefactor. When questioned as to who she thought she was—how she had come by the name of Beecham—she felt inclined to answer bitterly: "Do not call me by my name. It would be more convenient to call me by a number, as I am told the prisoners are called. Let me say I am number 18 or 24."

Mr. Standish still held an ever-present if somewhat dim place in the background of Meg's consciousness. It was a quaint half-goblin remembrance. The link between them seemed sundered forever. She had never heard from him since their parting. To Ursula alone she had spoken of that solitary time, of the friend who had been kind to her, and of the fashion-plate which had been sacred to her as her mother's portrait. To her alone she had shown her treasured presents. One day Ursula suggested that her mysterious protector was Mr. Standish. That the stern old gentleman was perhaps a guardian appointed by this friend in his absence. Meg had disclaimed the possibility. Yet the thought that he might be lingered in her mind. As a child loves wonderland, so she dwelt upon Ursula's suggestion. She reasoned herself out of it. She laughed at it, yet it remained. Was he not the only one who had cared for her in her unsheltered childhood?

"Describe him to me," Ursula had once asked.

"I cannot," Meg answered. "It is strange. I can remember a tie he wore—dark-blue, dotted over with tiny horseshoes; and I remember a pair of slippers he had, with big red roses on the toes. I remember his hands, and the color of his hair."

"And you can't remember his face?" Ursula said in tones of disappointment.

"Perhaps if I saw him I might," answered Meg reflectively. "It is so long ago, I have a very dim recollection of his features. They beamed with kindness, and he was kind to me." And then she would tell again the many kind things he had done, the memory of which she held sacred. "Ah," she continued, "I used to be unable to think and speak of those things without tears, but now you see my eyes are quite dry."

Once Meg asked Mr. Fullbloom if Mr. Standish was her guardian. The elderly lawyer she had once known was dead. His brother was now the representative of her unknown benefactor. He alone visited her from the outside world. The solicitor chuckled, as if he were amazingly tickled by this question, but he answered it neither in the affirmative nor the negative.

Mr. Horace Fullbloom was cheery and gray-headed; his sparkling brown eyes were surrounded by crinkles, suggestive of puckers made by laughter rather than by age. His appearance suggested a mischievous humor. Like his brother, he was a bit of a dandy. He also wore a frilled shirt, an impressive bloodstone ring on his little finger, and he sported a silver snuffbox. The solicitor was a favorite with the girls. His cynicism was the sunshine of cynicism. He chaffed them with paternal familiarity, watching them with amused benevolence. He seemed to regard them as belonging to a species not deserving any serious thought or treatment. Meg especially interested him. He always questioned her kindly about herself, and apparently relished the little tiffs that marked their intercourse.

These tiffs were caused by Meg's endeavors to find out the name of her mysterious benefactor, and by the humorous banter with which the solicitor evaded her curiosity. She had dreams of that human providence who stood between her and destitution. Every noble personality she heard or read of became associated in Meg's mind with the thought of her guardian hero. The banter with which Mr. Fullbloom met her inquiries did not prevent Meg from waiting and watching for the feverish moment when she would again question him. Was it the stern old gentleman she remembered who twice had appeared to her? If it were, what was his name? If it were not, who was it, then?

To the teasing humor with which the solicitor asked her why she wanted so much to know, she answered, "Because I am grateful."

"But gratitude, my dear," said Mr. Fullbloom, tapping his snuffbox, "wants an object. Suppose I were to tell you it was the big stone figure on the gate, or some old parchment will and testament that is your guardian. What then? Would you feel grateful to those bloodless patrons?"

"I would be grateful to one who remembered and thought of me were he living or dead," said Meg.

"Perhaps if he be alive he is a gruff, disagreeable old curmudgeon; you might be afraid of him—you might not like him!"

Meg was not to be baffled by such answers. She wanted to know who it was she had a right to love and be grateful to. It was such pain to her also to live among people who kept wondering who she was.

More than once she put into the solicitor's hands a letter, that she asked him to deliver to her unknown friend; but to these missives, that he invariably took away with him, Mr. Fullbloom never brought an answer. To her demand, had he delivered her letters, Mr. Fullbloom returned tantalizing answers. One day he admitted that he had put them all, every one, into the pillar post.

"But not as they were, without an address?" Meg asked in consternation.

"That was no concern of mine. I posted them," said Mr. Fullbloom.

"But where did my letters go?" she cried.

"Perhaps one went to Surrey; perhaps another found its way to York Minster; perhaps a third was carried by fate to its rightful owner," the solicitor replied with a chuckle, and eyes twinkling with the light of mischief. With a little burst of anger, Meg told him that if he would not tell her who her protector was she would rather not see him; it was so painful not to know to whom she owed all this gratitude.

After this scene a long interval elapsed, during which Mr. Fullbloom did not appear; till inconsistently Meg began to long for him to come and visit her again.

It was the eve of the Easter holidays. The school was breaking up. Meg had formed a resolution. This resolution helped her to bear the pain that always accompanied the approach of the holidays. The eager plans she heard her comrades discussing were ever an occasion of pain to her sensitive nature, bringing her loneliness home more keenly.

The gentle independence that now marked Meg's manner had grown upon her of late; the stern necessity of self-support that, since her childhood, had governed her thoughts and actions, had become the ruling instinct of her life. She had determined to be no longer a burden to her protector, and the resolve heightened her spirits. Dreaming is the employment of the idle, and Meg's life was one of action.

If something of the vividness that had distinguished her glance and expression in childhood seemed to have passed away, it was rather subdued or merged in a look, as of a habit of thought now usual to her. Meg's appearance was a matter of discussion in the school; some called her beautiful, others vowed she was plain. Her soft, silky "no color" hair—

"mousey hair" Ursula called it—went charmingly with her complexion; it obtruded somewhat heavily over her forehead, for she was inclined to be careless about her dress. Her beauty was of the sort that you do not think of analyzing. It grew upon the beholder, who invariably discovered that her features possessed beauty of form, and that the whole physiognomy had the charm that is magnetic.

Meg had been contemplating writing to Mr. Fullbloom to tell him the resolve she had taken, when his presence was announced in the drawing-room.

"Well, my dear," said the solicitor, taking her two hands in his, "here I am. I did not dare to show myself before I could communicate news. You commanded me the last time I saw you not to appear in your presence until I brought you tidings of your guardian."

"I was sorry I said that," replied Meg. "I have missed you. I did not think you would obey me so implicitly."

"Not after such a definite command!" Eh? exclaimed the solicitor, jerking his head on one side and surveying her with his superficially smiling glance. "Well, now, what news of yourself, little lady?" he continued, leading her to a chair and sitting down beside her.

"I have passed my examination," said Meg. "I am now at the head of the school."

Mr. Fullbloom put his hand on his heart and bowed.

"A modern Aspasia!" he replied as Meg paused, and seemed to hesitate. "Come," he went on, "when is our tiff to begin? I must have my tiff about the great Unknown."

"No," said Meg gently, "we shall have no more tiffs. I have made up my mind I will ask no more questions; and if possible, I shall cease wondering concerning myself. Whoever my benefactor may be, I am grateful to him—grateful from my heart. I wish I could prove my gratitude to him. I wish it so much that I cannot but think it will be granted to me to do so some day."

"Perhaps it will—and sooner than you think," exclaimed Mr. Fullbloom. "Ha! ha!" he went on tantalizingly, the flicker of mischief alight in his eyes as Meg looked up inquiringly. "You have just been saying you would not wonder any more.

"You would not be curious. Ha! ha! Mrs. Blue Beard, you would pry into any forbidden closet—you know you would—to find out that secret."

"No," repeated Meg, "I will not be curious any more. There must be some reason—some reason that I ought to respect. You will, I know, tell my kind friend, who he or she may be, that I am grateful; also, that I have taken a great resolve."

"Indeed!" said Fullbloom with evident enjoyment. "May I ask what it is?"

"I will not be dependent any longer. I am going to earn my own livelihood," replied Meg.

"How valorous we are, all of a sudden!" said Mr. Fullbloom, chuckling as if immensely tickled by the idea of Meg earning her livelihood.

"No, not all of a sudden!" said Meg with energy. "I have long thought of it. My wishes, my dreams have long been to be independent; to be no longer a pensioner on the bounty of one whose very name is unknown to me. I am going to be a governess. Miss Reeves has heard of a situation, the duties of which she thinks I am fitted to undertake—to teach three little girls in the country. The salary is thirty pounds. I won't be dependent any longer," repeated Meg with concentration.

"Miss Reeves and the three little girls go to Jericho!" cried Mr. Fullbloom. Then taking Meg's two hands in his paternal grasp, "My dear child," he said, "you have long wished to know your benefactor's name. To-morrow you will know it. You will not only know it, but you will be on a visit to him. He sends me to invite you down to stay at his place in the country."

"To-morrow!" repeated Meg. "On a visit to him! Who, then, is he?"

"Ha! ha!" cried Mr. Fullbloom gleefully. "All that fine assumption of having laid curiosity aside, where is it? No, no, no; not till to-morrow will you know anything about it."

"But where am I to go? Who am I to ask for?" cried Meg.

"Listen, my dear," explained Mr. Fullbloom, giving an occasional emphasis to his words by a pressure of Meg's hands. "You are to go to London first, then to the station of the North-Western Railway. Miss Reeves will go with you thus far; she will take a first-class ticket for you. You must take the train that leaves London at a quarter to three. I will be at Greywolds Station to meet you at half-past five. It takes over three hours to get to Greywolds."

Meg felt a sudden recoil as she realized how near she was to the meeting she had dreamed of so long.

"Don't trouble your little head about money. All that is settled. Miss Reeves will make the necessary preparations. You have nothing to do but attend to the farewells. I must be off now. I am going to Greywolds to-night. I have an appointment with your mysterious patron."

Mr. Fullbloom's eyes were brimming over with elvish laughter, as with another pressure of Meg's two hands he turned away. He left her standing silent and chill, under the impression of that sudden revulsion of feeling.

CHAPTER XX.

ARRIVAL.

Past stretches of meadowland and woodland, past undulating fields sleeping peacefully in the sunshine, past busy towns and reposeful hamlets sped the train bearing Meg to her unknown guardian's home. The solitude of the empty carriage oppressed her. The flurry of the farewells and the pain of sundered associations increased the timidity of her spirit, as she realized more vividly that she was hurrying she knew not whither to meet she knew not whom.

Meg had not yet recovered from the recoil she had experienced on hearing that she was so soon to meet her mysterious benefactor. As every moment lengthened the space that parted her from surroundings which, if not altogether sympathetic, had yet the sweetness of familiarity, the unknown future presented itself to her invested with a touch of fear. She combated this mood. Was she not hastening toward the human being who had shown solicitude toward her in her forlornness?

She felt almost sure that her protector would prove to be the stern stranger whom she had twice seen in her childhood, and yet there would drift up to her mind the possibility that Mr. Standish might turn out to be this unknown friend.

"I hope not," Meg said to herself, sudden shame overcoming her at the possibility of meeting so soon, and of owing so much to one upon whose personality her thoughts had dwelt so long. "I was a foolish sprite of a child when I cared for him. I am a young woman now," she murmured.

When she stepped out on the platform of the wayside station of Greywolds she looked about. Mr. Fullbloom was not there. No one appeared to be waiting for her. A farmer's cart and a private carriage were drawn up on the other side of the paling that separated the country station from the roadside. The single passenger who had alighted besides herself from the train got into the carriage and drove off; the cart after depositing a load of metal casks jogged away. Meg felt bewildered. If Mr. Fullbloom did not come for her, what was she to do? She had no money with which to pay her fare back. She did not know the name of the place to which to direct the porter to take her luggage after she had identified her modest trunk. The old sense of isolation so familiar to her in her schooldays paralyzed Meg, and her eyelids smarted, as if she were about to cry.

Suddenly a carriage drove up, the gate of the station was pushed open, and the dandified figure of Mr. Fullbloom came gayly forward.

"So, you have found your way," he said airily.

"I was afraid you had forgotten your appointment," Meg answered with dignity.

"I always associate this train and ladies with unpunctuality," the solicitor replied with unruffled equanimity.

Offering Meg his arm he led her out. Nervousness conquered every other feeling, even curiosity. She asked no questions as she perceived a carriage with two horses and liveried servants awaiting her. She stepped inside, sank back into the cushioned seat, with Mr. Fullbloom by her side. As she felt herself bowled along she gave a little gasp.

The solicitor was very chatty. He inquired after her journey. He asked details of the parting with schoolfellows. He pointed out pretty bits in the landscape. Meg could not follow what he said; a longing for silence was upon her. She wished with all her heart her companion would hold his tongue and let her think and realize.

Presently the carriage drove through gates, thrown open to let it pass in. The way lay under an avenue of trees. A park stretched to right and left. As Meg looked round she felt sure this stately domain could not belong to William Standish.

"This is Greywolds Manor," said Mr. Fullbloom with a chuckle, pointing to a solid gray pile flanked with turrets at either end. "What do you think of your new home?"

Meg did not answer. Now that she knew for certain it was not the friend of her childhood who would welcome her when she alighted she was aware of an inconsistent disappointment. There came a sudden chill in the air. The owner of this lordly place would not understand her. Everything seemed gigantic, repellent. The trees threw too much shadow, the sunshine was too bright, the massive house too large for homeliness.

"Sir Malcolm Loftdale is the proprietor of this place. Now the mystery is out. You know the name of your benefactor," chuckled Mr. Fullbloom, the signals of mischievous enjoyment alight in his eyes.

The carriage had drawn up before the door of the mansion. Meg descended; she was aware of a discreet-looking elderly man helping to gather together her loose traps, of a respectable-looking dame in an impressive black silk gown coming forward to meet her.

"This is Mrs. Jarvis, Sir Malcolm's trusty housekeeper. I cannot leave you in better hands. Good-by, my dear," said Mr. Fullbloom. Kissing his finger tips and spreading them in the air, he disappeared through a side door.

Meg followed the housekeeper up a softly-carpeted staircase, fragrant with the perfume of flowers. She was vaguely aware of statues in niches, of limpid pictures dreaming on the walls. A knight of old entering an enchanted castle could not have felt more strange and bewildered, or could not have summoned more desperate courage than did Meg as she moved up that grand staircase.

She was ushered into a pretty bedroom, hexagon shaped. Through the windows looking out on the park at different angles poured the mellow light of the late afternoon. Meg, at the request of a trim maid in a dark gown and dainty muslin cap and apron, gave up the key of her trunk, painfully realizing as she did so the slenderness and shabbiness of the wardrobe that would be exposed to this smart young woman's gaze. With brusque shyness she answered the housekeeper's bland expressions of hospitality and exhortations to rest. In a trice the deft-handed, nimble-footed attendant had disposed of the modest stock of wearing apparel in wardrobes and drawers, and arranged on the tables the books, desk, and cheap knickknacks—parting presents from some of Meg's school friends; after which she disappeared with the housekeeper, to return after a few moments carrying a delicate porcelain and silver five o'clock solitaire tea-service, which she deposited on a table by Meg's side. Then the trim attendant, in tones as respectful as if Meg's belongings had revealed her to be a duchess, asked if she could do anything more for Miss Beecham. On receiving a timorous negative she announced that dinner was served at seven-thirty; that the dressing bell would sound at seven. Could she help Miss Beecham to dress? "No, thank you," replied Meg hastily; "I am accustomed to dress myself."

With a sense of relief Meg heard the door close, and reflected that probably until dinner-time she would be left alone.

She poured herself out a cup of tea and looked round the room. It was a charming little chamber. Its shape showed that it was placed in a tower. On all sides she was surrounded by sky and trees. After awhile she set about making a journey of discovery. One of the windows was over the mantelpiece; she tried to find how the flue of the chimney went to allow of this quaint arrangement. A bookcase stood in a corner; its shelves held a delightful selection of books. A water-color drawing representing a stormy sea, another of a peaceful and Arcadian scene, hung on the walls. Two miniatures—one of Queen Elizabeth in an immense ruffle, another of Mary, Queen of Scots—adorned a recess. The bed was large, with two pillows; the coverlid and hangings, of delicate sea-blue damask, matched the curtains at the windows. An electric bell was placed near the bed. Meg thought it was the prettiest, coziest little chamber she had ever seen, and her spirits rose.

She was still in a kind of half reverie when the gong sounded, and looking at the clock, she perceived that the short hand pointed to seven.

Taking out her white muslin gown, Meg began to array herself with care. She had never devoted much thought to her toilet before, but she was eager to please her benefactor. She coiled her brown hair smoothly round her head, and fastened a red rose in her bodice. Then she waited till the gong sounded again.

Timidity once more overcame her as she descended the grand staircase; realizing at every step more keenly that the moment had come when she would be ushered into the presence of her benefactor. Two footmen in plush and gold lace stood on either side of an open door; this was the room in which her host awaited her.

Meg paused on the threshold. A somewhat short elderly man in evening dress stood near the table. This was no familiar figure; but she remained where she was, overwhelmed with emotion, looking dumbly at this protector of her forlorn youth. She could not speak for her beating heart. Her shyness was enhanced by the silence of her host. He did not advance to greet her; he did not stretch out a hand of welcome. He stood close to a chair in a somewhat deferential attitude. Then suddenly Meg recognized him to be the butler who had received her in the hall on her arrival. She had not identified him in her fright.

With a painful sense of the absurdity of her mistake she took the seat he placed for her and looked hurriedly round the table. The flower and fruit-decked expanse, the white cloth, the plate and delicate glass, glowed rosily under the crimson-shaded suspension lamp; no second cover was laid, no other chairs near the board. She was to dine alone.

Meg had scarcely realized this when a plateful of soup was placed before her, and she felt the two magnificent lackeys standing on either side of her chair, watching as she dipped the spoon and raised it to her lips. The thought that she was to eat her dinner under the inspection of this frigid and observant gaze struck her with palsied nervousness. She upset a tumbler as she stretched her hand for the salt-cellar; she helped herself to everything that was offered to her by her attendants; she allowed the butler without protest to fill the glasses at her side with claret, hock, and champagne, and let the beverages stand there untasted. In the awful silence she started when the door opened. After awhile the tension of her nervousness was relieved by a freakish fancy. What a good story it would make to tell the girls in the dormitory! How she had sat in a skimpy muslin dress in this splendid room, hung round with family portraits which seemed to be watching her; of the sumptuous repast served to her alone; of the obsequiousness of the servant men; how terrified she had been; with what clumsiness she had behaved, and with what attempts at dignity!

There came a moment at last when, every trace of heavier diet having been removed, the servants retired, after having placed the dessert and three decanters of wine before Meg. She drew a breath of relief as she made sure that she was alone. A girlish love of fruit came over her, and she helped herself to a bunch of grapes. She remembered she had once heard the story of a girl who for a day had been mistaken for a queen. The people cheered her, the courtiers obeyed her slightest wish. Meg smiled as she thought this girl must have felt as she felt to-night.

She glanced around as she ate her grapes. The table made a patch of brilliancy in the long room, the corners of which remained dusky. Gleaming frames caught the light of the suspension lamp, and here and there revealed the superb apparel of the dignified full-length men and women gazing down upon her from the walls. As Meg's eyes traveled slowly round this stately company she was vaguely revolving in her mind how she would summon up courage to leave this room and make her way back to her own.

Presently her eyes rested on what looked like a blank framed space at the furthest end of the apartment. She could not distinguish the cause of this effect. It puzzled her, so she rose from her chair and drew nearer. She found it was a picture with its face turned to the wall.

The discovery affected her like the touch of a spectral hand. That disgraced canvas riveted her attention. What did it mean? She looked away; but the spell continued to work, and once more she drew near. The sight of its disgrace brought a piteous feeling. It looked like an outcast in the midst of this painted pageantry of splendid men and women.

Whose face was it thus turned away? Was it that of a man or of a woman? Meg felt as if she would give anything to know. Everything else faded in interest near the story of that picture. She tried vainly to discover a trace of revealing outline. The fascination grew too strong. She got up on a chair and tried with all her strength to turn the picture round and get a glimpse. She had succeeded in moving it slightly when she heard behind her the door open.

Meg dropped her hold of the frame and turned round.

The housekeeper was standing on the threshold looking at her aghast.

"Miss Beecham, what are you doing?"

"I was trying to get a peep at this picture," said Meg, jumping down. "Why is its face turned to the wall?"

Mrs. Jarvis shook her head. "Why, miss, it would be worth a servant's place in this house to turn that picture round. Sir Malcolm Loftdale has forbidden the name of the person whose portrait that is to be mentioned. He never comes into this room. I am sure it is because of that picture."

"Indeed; I am sorry," said Meg in some confusion.

"I could tell you all about that picture, Miss Beecham. I have been in this house these thirty years, and I was there the day it was turned to the wall. It was a day I'll never forget—not so long as I live; but it's laid upon me not to tell," went on the housekeeper, who looked packed with mystery.

"Do not think I would wish you to tell me," exclaimed Meg hurriedly. "I would not—not on any account." Then she asked with abrupt transition: "Shall I see Sir Malcolm Loftdale to-night?"

"No, Miss Beecham, not to-night. Sir Malcolm sent me down to ask you to excuse him. He is old, miss, and not strong. He hopes that you will forgive his not welcoming you himself, and that you will make yourself at home."

"Thank Sir Malcolm Loftdale for me, and say that I feel very grateful to him for his hospitality," Meg replied, relieved yet vaguely nettled by her host's neglect.

"Coffee is served in the drawing-room, Miss Beecham."

"Thank you; but I think I shall return to my room," said Meg.

She hurried up the staircase. A confused pain seemed to haunt the surrounding splendor. It oppressed her as might the scent of flowers in a room of death.

When she opened the door of her pretty room, the sea-green silk curtains of which had been drawn, the daintiness and comfort contrasted pleasantly with the alien magnificence outside, saddened as it was by a jarring note of brooding grief. A black cat had found its way in, and came forward to meet Meg with tail uplifted and a welcoming purr. The homeliness of the scene revived her drooping spirits.

CHAPTER XXI.

SIR MALCOLM LOFTDALE.

Meg had more than once explored the house and the grounds. She had performed the pilgrimage under the expansive wing of Mrs. Jarvis; she had wandered alone over the mansion and rambled through the park, feeling delight in the old-world charm of the place. The touch of tragic mystery brought into the atmosphere by the picture on which a ban had been laid now added to the spell of its fascination. The lofty rooms, with somber gilt or painted ceilings; the faded tapestries and brocaded hangings; the dusky tones of the furniture, upon which the sunbeams fell with an antique glow, appeared to her steeped in the mystery of associations. Every room seemed a chapter in an unknown story, the thought of which kindled her fancy. The park, with its lengthening vistas, its sylvan retreats, and patriarchal trees, a branch of the silver river sweeping through its stately alleys; the stretches of lawns, the flower-gardens, the glass structures in which bloomed a tropical vegetation, enchanted her.

It was like living in a picture, she thought, to live amid such peaceful, beautiful, finely ordered surroundings, whose past haunted them like a presence. After the crude and noisy bustle of immature possibilities to which she was accustomed, the wearied splendors of this domain came to her as a revelation of novel possibilities in the setting of life.

A week had elapsed, Meg had almost grown accustomed to the place, and yet she had not seen its owner. She had at first begun every morning by asking Mrs. Jarvis if there was a probability of her seeing Sir Malcolm Loftdale during the course of the day, but the housekeeper on each occasion had given an evasive answer, and Meg now asked no more. She might have felt wounded at this breach of hospitality had not the behavior of the servants precluded all idea of a slight being offered to her. They paid her obsequious attention, they obeyed her slightest expressed wish. She might have imagined herself the queen of the domain. The solitude, the homage paid to her, the regard for her comfort, reminded her of a fairy tale where the host remains unseen and the heroine lives in splendor and isolation. She wondered often why her benefactor kept himself thus sternly secluded. She began to think it could not be the old gentleman she had seen in her childhood; why should he avoid her? If it were a stranger was it because of some unsightly physical affliction, some form of mental derangement? was it a brooding melancholy that caused him morbidly to shrink from contact with outsiders? A longing to be of comfort mingled with the curiosity she felt concerning her mysterious host.

One late afternoon as she rambled in the park she saw, framed in by trees as in a picture, the figure of a tall, slender, white-haired gentleman walking toward her. She recognized him at once. It was the mysterious stranger, twice met in her childhood. He held his head high. What a head it was! There was an eagle cast of physiognomy, a chill expression in the eyes, a hardness on the lips. He wore a country suit and carried a heavy gold-headed stick; a diamond stud on a jeweled seal caught the light and shone. These little details curiously impressed themselves upon Meg. She stopped, asking herself if this was the master of the house?

The stranger glanced toward her, lifted his hat, and with an old-world salute passed on. Meg determined not to look after him; but she could not resist the temptation, and turning round she saw him ascending the steps of the house. On questioning the housekeeper, Meg found that the picturesque old gentleman was Sir Malcolm Loftdale.

Next morning Meg was standing arranging some flowers in the window of the little room she had chosen for her morning retreat—it looked out on a pleasant side alley of the grounds in the center of which stood a sun dial—when the door suddenly opened, and the gentleman she had seen in the park on the previous evening entered unannounced. He did not advance beyond the threshold, but he closed the door after him and kept one hand on the handle. He did not extend the other in greeting.

At sight of him Meg's heart fluttered, and she acknowledged by a flurried inclination of her head his stately bow.

He was handsomer than she had imagined him to be; but the light of his stern blue eye remained cold, and there was a remoteness in the steady glance that he fixed upon her.

"I beg you, Miss Beecham, to excuse me for not having welcomed you before," he said in a voice of cold courtesy. "I trust you will forgive me for exercising a privilege age is apt freely to indulge near youth—that of following the usual routine of life. I am a solitary, my life is organized for loneliness."

"You have been most kind, sir," muttered Meg, in a tumult of timidity.

"My servants have received strict orders to attend to your comfort. I hope they have been attentive?"

"They have been very attentive," replied Meg.

"I fear the days may seem to drag heavily for you, Miss Beecham," the old gentleman resumed, without a shadow of softening in the coldness of his voice or the scrutiny of his glance. "I have thought—to relieve their tedium—that you might like a horse. I will have one broken for your use. There are pretty rides about."

"I do not know how to ride, sir," said Meg, touched and bewildered by the thoughtfulness and repellent manner of her host.

"My old groom would teach you; he is a most trustworthy and respectable man," said Sir Malcolm.

"Thank you sir," said Meg. Then with desperate courage, as her benefactor seemed about to retire, she added breathlessly: "I should not feel lonely, sir—not—if you would let me be with you a little—if you would let me read for you, or do something for you. You have been so good to me all those years."

The old gentleman bowed hastily; the expression of his cold glance seemed to grow colder as he replied: "I assure you, Miss Beecham, you need feel yourself under no obligation to me for what I have done. It is very little."

"Little! It was everything to me!" said Meg hurriedly, her voice trembling with restrained emotion. "You twice saved me from a wretched fate. But for you, sir, as you told me on that evening you took me back to school, I would have been as uncared for as a workhouse child."

"I wish, if you will allow me distinctly to state my wishes, that allusion to the past be dropped between us. I can repeat only that you are under no obligation," replied her host, his thin lips remaining tense in their cruel firmness of line, his glance courteously repellent. "When the case was pointed out to me it became my plain duty to do what I did."

"I do not understand; I only know that if you had not been good to me I should have been ignorant and homeless," answered Meg with reckless iteration.

There was a pause, Sir Malcolm frowned, then he said with the same impassible frigidity:

"If you choose, Miss Beecham, to consider that you are under a debt of gratitude to me, allow me to say that you will express it in the manner most agreeable to me by never referring to the subject."

Bowing once more with that impassible fineness of mien, the old gentleman opened the door and disappeared.

Meg felt crushed as by some physical blow. The gratitude that she had harbored in her heart till it was filled to bursting all those years was thrown back upon it, and the pain stifled her. She realized her loneliness as she never had realized it before. She wandered blindly out into the park, and for the first time, in the heart of nature, she felt like an outcast. She rebelled against the isolation to which her benefactor would condemn her. It felt like an insult.

To be grateful to those who are good to us is a sacred right. He had no authority to take from her this God-given privilege. After awhile she grew calmer, but a melancholy fell over her such as she had never known.

Day succeeded day, and the intercourse between Meg and her host remained but little changed. She watched him curiously whenever she had the opportunity. She came to know his habits. A young man was closeted with him for some hours every morning. Mrs. Jarvis told Meg he was Sir Malcolm's secretary, and read the papers to him, as the baronet's eyesight was beginning to fail. He had lodgings in the village.

Sir Malcolm rode out alone, walked alone, took his meals alone, spent his evenings alone. Occasionally some elderly country squires called at the house; but there was apparently no intimacy between the baronet and his neighbors. Meg often watched her host wandering about the park; there was an alley he haunted. As he paced backward and forward, his hands behind his back, his tall figure, slender almost to gauntness, clothed in the somewhat old-fashioned costume he affected, his white hair shining like spun glass about his pale, high-featured face, she thought he looked like a ghost which had stepped down out of one of the pictures. Little by little she grew to feel an intense interest in that stately specter.

Whenever they met Sir Malcolm was courteous and cold. Sometimes he passed her by with that old-world salute; oftener he stopped to inquire after her comfort, to offer with distant interest suggestions for her amusement. He recommended her books to read; he once pointed out to her the parts of the house to which historical interest was attached.

He attracted and repelled Meg. She was always in a fright when she was near him. His glance withered every impulse to pass the distance he imposed between them. A chill air seemed around him, as might be round an iceberg. The look of power on his face, the suggestion his appearance gave of a strong, self-contained personality, possessed for her the same sort of fascination as the flash and iridescence of an iceberg that will not melt. The interest Meg felt for her host kept pace with her fear. She always connected that picture turned to the wall with his history and his character. There it was always in presence, and yet under apparently some black disgrace.

Away from Sir Malcolm, she would indulge a zeal to win his regard, to conquer it. Watching his solitary pacings to and fro, a pity would fill her heart for the lonely man who had been so good to her. In his presence came the chill, checking every expression of emotion. Sometimes when she met his glance she fancied her benefactor disliked her.

The sadness deepened upon Meg—the sadness of a sensitive nature condemned to isolation. The inaction of her days wearied her. She looked back with a touch of nostalgia on the busy schooldays, and mourned anew for Elsie, who had allowed her to give love. Meg's pride also rebelled against eating the bread of idleness under her benefactor's roof: that gentle independence had grown a sort of second nature with her.

One morning she was aware of a certain flurry through the house. Mrs. Jarvis told her that Sir Malcolm's secretary had been called away suddenly to London on important family business, and that the master was left with his papers alone.

Meg received the information in silence. For a few moments after the housekeeper left she stood still, thinking. Once or twice she walked to the room and came back irresolute. She at last went determinedly out of the room and made her way to the library, where Sir Malcolm spent the greater part of his time indoors.

She knocked, but scarcely waited for permission to open the door. Walking swiftly in before he could recognize her, she stood by Sir Malcolm's chair.

"I have come to ask if I may read to you, sir, in the absence of Mr. Robinson?" she said in the smooth, quick voice of mastered timidity.

He looked up surprised, and rose.

"I could not accept it of you," he said with a bow.

"Why not?" she asked with breathless gentleness.

"Did Mrs. Jarvis suggest to you to come?" he said with a quick frown, an evidence of irritation he suppressed at once.

"No," said Meg. "I heard Mr. Robinson had left, and I hoped that you would let me take his place."

"That would be impossible. I would not lay such a tax upon any lady," he said with courteous definiteness of accent and manner.

"Why will you not let me read to you?" asked Meg pleadingly.

"Because," he answered, with an attempt at lightness of tone that did not yet take from its distance and firmness, "young ladies do not care for politics, and politics alone interest me."

"They would interest me if I read them for you," said Meg with timid persistence.

"Allow me to beg you to put into the balance against this plea the argument that it would be disagreeable to me," Sir Malcolm replied, with a directness the brutality of which was veiled by the stately tone of dismissal in his voice and manner. "And the spirit that impelled you to undertake the task would make it all the more painful."

As Meg did not answer he continued:

"Excuse the frankness of my refusal. I thank you, nevertheless, for the offer."

He glanced toward the door, and as she moved away he advanced to open it for her; but Meg paused on her way. Her spirit was up; the fear that hitherto had quelled her before him fell from her. She had grown suddenly irritated at his invincible coldness. She would expose herself to no more rebuffs.

"May I ask you, sir, to be so kind as to spare me a moment? I have a request to make."

"Certainly," he replied, turning back; he sat down and pointed to a chair near his. But Meg remained standing.

Embarrassment, resolution kept her motionless with a touch of angular rigidity in her pose. Her voice, unsteady at first, grew more controlled as she went on:

"Before leaving school I had an offer of a situation as governess to three young children. You were kind enough, sir, to ask me on a visit. I thank you for the hospitality you have shown me. I think my visit must now come to an end. With your permission I shall inquire if the place is still vacant, and take it if it be."

"Why do you want to go, Miss Beecham?" said Sir Malcolm. "Are you not comfortable here?"

"Comfortable, yes," said Meg. She paused as if hesitating, then she added brusquely, "I do not think I care much for comfort."

There was something primitive, almost childish, in Meg's manner; but it gave the impression of the strength rather than of the weakness of childhood. It came with a freshness that was as the scent of the flower rather than that of the toilet perfume.

Meg's mood seemed to pique the old gentleman; he looked curiously at her, almost as if for the first time he recognized in her an individuality.

"You do not care for comfort. That is a great source of independence," he observed.

"I wish to be independent," said Meg with gentle spirit.

"You are proud. It is a spirit that should be repressed," he answered.

"I do not know if I am proud," replied Meg, her low, feeling voice under evident restraint. "I know it pains me to be here receiving everything, giving nothing in return."

"What could you give?" he asked with a slight contraction of his hard lips.

"I could give proofs of what I feel—gratitude," she said.

"I have explained I do not want gratitude," he replied with chill distinctness. "I do not either wish to receive it or to inspire it."

"You cannot help my feeling it," Meg broke out with spirit and with a vivid glance; "that is beyond your control. You may condemn me to silence and to apparent apathy, but the gratitude is here all the same; and because I cannot express it, it becomes a burden and hurts me."

There was a pause, during which Sir Malcolm continued to look at Meg with that new look of curiosity, as if for the first time he recognized her as a personality.

"Am I to understand," he said slowly, "that you wish to leave my house because I do not care for any allusion to be made between us of the part I have taken in defraying the cost of your education?"

Meg made a quick gesture. "Because you will let me do nothing for you, and also because I want to be independent. I would never wish to leave you if I could be of service to you—never; but as you will not let me, I ask you to let me go and earn my own living."

Sir Malcolm bowed his head. "I understand; you do not wish to be dependent upon me for your maintenance."

"No, sir."

"Suppose," resumed her host after a pause, "I were to feel disposed to accept the offer you just now made to me, to replace Mr. Robinson during his absence, would you allow me to do so?"

Meg gave an exclamation of acceptance.

MEG READS THE MORNING PAPERS TO SIR MALCOLM.—Page 255.

"Understand me," said the old man with deliberate distinctness, looking full at Meg. "It is a business proposal. I still maintain my point. I do not want gratitude. If I accept your services, it is on the condition that you will accept a remuneration."

Meg colored. For a moment she knit her brows, then she said with effort, "I shall accept the chance of being of service to you under any condition, sir, that you may name."

"So be it, then," said the baronet.

At a sign from him Meg sat down and took up the *Times*. "Where shall I begin, sir?" she asked.

"With the first leader, if you please," he replied with an inclination of the head, crossing his knees, and composing himself to listen.

Meg read, mastering her nervousness with a strong effort of will. Once or twice she looked up and caught his eyes fixed upon her, with that new curiosity in their glance that seemed to humanize their expression.

After she had read the *Times*, the political leaders of the *Standard*, and selections from its foreign correspondence under Sir Malcolm's directions, a third paper remained—the local organ apparently—the *Greywolds Mercury*. At the murmured injunction of her auditor, "The leader, if you please," Meg once more set upon her task.

The article handled a book upon the rights of property which had lately appeared and was making a stir. As Meg read the opening paragraph her voice faltered and hesitated. She was reading a fierce attack upon Sir Malcolm Loftdale.

She looked up distressed and flurried. The old man set his jaw. "Go on," he said, and Meg continued. She could scarcely follow the drift of what she read for sympathy with the pain she was inflicting upon her benefactor. She confusedly gathered that Sir Malcolm had raised rents in order to get rid of certain tenants on his estate; that the compensation he gave his ejected cottagers might appear to justify the proceeding, which nevertheless remained in the eyes of the writer of the article an infamous cruelty.

"I think this will suffice for to-day, Miss Beecham," said the baronet, when she had read to the end.

She rose as he spoke. She noticed he looked paler. "Is there no letter, sir, that I can write for you?" asked Meg.

"None this morning, I thank you," he replied with that fine air of dismissal which awed Meg. He preceded her to the door, and held it open for her to pass out.

CHAPTER XXII.

THE EDITOR OF THE "GREYWOLDS MERCURY."

Morning after morning Meg appeared at her post. She was punctual. As the clock struck ten her knock sounded at the library door, and she glided in. The greeting between her employer and herself was always the same—a formal and courtly bow from him, an inclination of the head and low "Good morning, sir," from her. Then she would begin to read. She knew the order in which he liked to listen to the contents of the various journals. Sometimes also Meg remained to write letters. She had rebelled at first against the business contract her benefactor had proposed to her; she liked it well enough now that she had entered upon it. The touch of frigidity it brought into the more emotional relationship of gratitude with which she regarded him imparted definiteness to their intercourse. The somewhat elaborate courtesy with which he treated her lent a charm to service.

On Wednesday and Saturday the *Greywolds Mercury* appeared among the papers to be read. Its columns usually contained an attack, covert or personal, against Sir Malcolm Loftdale. Sometimes he was mentioned by name; sometimes he was alluded to in pointed and unmistakable terms as "a large landed proprietor living in unsympathetic isolation." In his dealings toward his tenants he was represented as a tyrant, not so much actively as passively; and "passive injustice," the writer maintained, "is worse than active, for it leaves no hope behind."

Meg felt a flame of indignant protest rising against this persistent abuse. She would have skipped the censure so relentlessly pursuing the old man, who listened in silence with jaw set and lips compressed; but he always detected the attempt, and bade her "go on" in a voice so stern that its tone stopped the reluctant quaver in hers. Meg knew that her auditor, who never offered a word of remonstrance or vouchsafed an exclamation as she read, suffered from these scathing attacks. He looked paler and feebler, she thought, during the day, and wandered with more piteous aimlessness about the park.

One hot Wednesday afternoon she came upon him asleep in a garden chair in the sunshine. The feebleness of his aspect strangely appealed to Meg. He looked so frail and pale. The pride of his appearance was relaxed. The colorless features, the delicate hands loosely crossed, might have been modeled in wax. In the immobility of sleep the face had a tragic cast. Meg thought it looked like that of one dead, who in life had suffered beyond the ordinary lot of man. Pity and indignation that one so old and stricken should be made to suffer stirred Meg's heart. For a moment she looked upon her benefactor, and then she turned away with moistened eyes.

Meg was no dreamer. She was of an active nature. As she walked feverishly about the grounds she found herself remonstrating in imagination with this venomous persecutor of one who had cast a spell of interest over her, and to whom she owed so much. She sometimes stopped in her walk to complete some angry appeal. Suddenly a daring thought arose in her mind. She would call upon this man, and in the strength of a just cause she would meet him face to face without anger, and tell him the injury he was doing to an old man's life. Would she dare to do it? She did not know the editor's name, but she had noticed that letters published in the paper were simply addressed to him in his official capacity. She knew where to find the office of the *Greywolds Mercury*. She had seen it one day that she had had occasion to visit the market town two miles distant. After the first flash of courage her spirit failed as she approached the gate. She hesitated. She thought of that newspaper in the library, and went back and read the article again. Again her indignation blazed up. Holding the paper in her hand she set out on her mission. As she walked she read over portions of the article to keep her zeal warm. Thus she proceeded on her way, filled with her theme, yet faltering.

She reached the town, and turned into the High Street where the office stood. She easily recognized it by the posters outside and the advertisements in the windows. Meg entered the shabby interior with a desperate effort, and while trembling, yet full of moral courage, impelled to act by what seemed to be a duty. A clerk sat at a desk; a small boy was posting and rolling up the papers. It was the dingiest corner from which a thunderbolt could be launched.

"I want to see the editor," she said brusquely.

"He is busy, miss," answered the clerk, surveying her slowly over his spectacles.

"I want to see him on important business," said Meg determinedly, trying to look unabashed.

"What name shall I say?" asked the clerk.

"Miss Beecham; but he will not know me," replied Meg.

The clerk disappeared, and returned after a moment to say the editor would be glad to see the lady.

They climbed a narrow, dusty flight of stairs that led to a glass door. It was opened by her guide, who ushered her into a room that impressed her as a medley of papers and books. A man, who had been sitting before a large table, rose at her entrance. She perceived that he was tall and broad-shouldered, that his countenance was energetic and expressive, and his glance brilliant. The lower part of his face was hidden by a reddish beard; the closely-cropped hair was of a darker and less ruddy hue. He bowed to her.

"Are you the editor of the *Greywolds Mercury*?" she asked, making another desperate effort to conquer her shyness.

"I am," he answered.

"If anything appears in the paper that is unjust it is to you one must appeal?"

"Certainly. I hope nothing of this kind has appeared," he answered. His tone was curt, his voice deep and not inharmonious.

"It is because something unjust has appeared, and has been repeated, that I have called upon you," said Meg.

"Indeed! Would you tell me the particulars? Pray, sit down," said the editor. If his manner had a certain *brusquerie* it was that of self-possession; it was characteristic of a man accustomed to speak to business men, and who could listen as well as talk.

He was dressed with a certain negligence, but with great neatness. Meg noticed, she knew not why, his large, well-shaped hand.

"There have been a number of articles upon Sir Malcolm Loftdale," began Meg.

The editor acknowledged the truth of this statement by an inclination of the head.

"I know Sir Malcolm well. I am staying at Greywolds Manor. I am taking the place of his secretary," said Meg, determinedly ignoring the shyness that, without chilling her indignation, yet threatened to overcome her under the scrutinizing glance of the editor. "I am under great obligations to Sir Malcolm, I owe him everything."

The editor bowed his head, but did not break the silence. He appeared to be waiting for more cogent reasons to be advanced. Meg felt to a certain degree baffled by his manner.

"You do not know how good he is," she resumed with energy, "and you represent him as unjust and tyrannical."

"You must remember the criticisms are upon Sir Malcolm in his public capacity of landlord and magistrate. They do not apply to him as a private individual," said the editor.

Meg made a movement as if repudiating this line of argument.

"A man cannot be one thing in his public capacity and another in his private relationship," she said quickly.

"I am afraid he can," answered the editor, with a smile distantly brightening his glance.

"I cannot believe it," said Meg with energy. "He is old and feeble. It is cruel to hurt him, and I know those attacks hurts him. He never says a word. He has never mentioned the subject to me. I watch him as I read aloud to him, and I think they will kill him."

"I think you exaggerate their importance," said the editor, averting his glance in which Meg thought she detected a sparkle of amusement. After a moment he resumed with seriousness. "You must understand me. I do not like to hurt your feelings, but this is a matter of principle with me. To put it plainly, Sir Malcolm Loftdale is a bad landlord, and in a public sense a bad man."

Meg gave an exclamation. "I do not believe it; I do not accept this statement. You misjudge him, You do not know him as I know him. He leads a lonely life and perhaps does not know."

"Exactly! That is one of the reasons that make him a bad landlord. He ignores the needs of his tenants by indulging his selfish love of loneliness, he becomes utterly unsympathetic. He cares nothing for the laborers who look to him for securing them the commonest rights, more decent dwellings, fair rents. And yet what wonder," continued the editor, turning his head away and speaking as if to himself, "that he should not care for them, when he did not care for his own son."

Meg thought of the picture with its face turned to the wall. She felt she touched a boundary that lay beyond her self-imposed task, and she rose.

"I see that I am making no way," she said in hurt accents. "I cannot influence you to abandon the cruel course you seem determined to pursue. Nothing remains for me to do but to apologize for having made the attempt, and to go."

"Indeed," said the editor, rising also, "I am sorry I should have given this wrong impression of the interest with which I have listened to your arguments in favor of Sir Malcolm Loftdale, and of your appeal against the censure pronounced upon him in the *Greywolds Mercury*. But, believe me, there are many upon his estate who daily talk of him more bitterly than I do; many who have been compelled to leave and to face ruin in already over-crowded cities after accepting his offer of compensation, which was a hard bargain driven on his side alone. You do not know, perhaps, the merits of the case against him. He turns his tenants out, if they are not punctual with their rents as soon as the law allows. In his selfish desire for isolation he allows no cottages to be built on his extensive estates. He has checked innocent amusements; barred the right of way. These sufferers represent the people. I shall not offend you by stating what I could of the class to which Sir Malcolm belongs. You see I have argued and discussed the matter fairly with you," continued the editor, checking the warmth of his tone.

"I cannot judge the case as you state it," said Meg with a pained frown. "I am sure it is one-sided." Then with gathering energy she went on: "Cannot you conceive that your continued persecution may drive him to worse acts? It is enough to make him shun his neighbors to be thus always held up to them as cruel and exacting. It is enough to make him wish to remove them from his sight when he knows that they are taught to revile him. I know that he is good. Take my case. I owe him everything; yet I have no claim upon him. Doubtless mine is not an isolated case. He may be helping many others in an obscure way. Noble natures shrink from publicity. I know he shrinks from being thanked. He will not allow me to thank him. It almost led to a misunderstanding between us when I tried to express to him my gratitude. You talk of his getting rid of tenants after giving them compensation. What is that suffering compared to the one you inflict upon him by these words that may sting to death?"

Meg's defense of her guardian was not logical, but it was of the heart, and womanly. She ignored all her antagonist's arguments, and saw everything colored by her emotions of the moment. The editor looked at her with a sort of half-amused amazement. Her vehemence was not to be answered by balanced sentences or editorial dignity.

"You are so good an advocate," he said, smiling, "that you almost incline me to be a convert."

"I wish I could convert you to believe in his goodness—to me, and perhaps to many others," said Meg, with the constraint of shy awkwardness upon her, as she accepted the homage of his softened mood.

"His kindness to you is all that I care for," said the editor, gallantly.

"Will you promise me not to write any more articles against him?" asked Meg, with the childlike almost primitive directness that occasionally distinguished her speech when greatly in earnest.

"I promise to remember your advocacy whenever I begin to write, or to think of Sir Malcolm Loftdale," answered the editor.

"You promise it?" repeated Meg.

"I promise it," said the editor.

After a pause of awkward hesitation Meg bowed and turned away. The editor held open the door for her, and she passed out of the dingy office.

As Meg walked home she was conscious of a certain light-heartedness. The interview had been, on the whole, antagonistic; yet the impression it left on her mind was pleasant. The editor was a stranger, and yet he almost seemed to her a friend. She could not account for a sense of trustfulness with which she felt inclined to regard him. There was nothing to justify this confidence, yet the impression remained.

CHAPTER XXIII.

FRIEND OR FOE.

The impression, for which she could give no reason, that this stranger was a friend remained with Meg. When on the following Wednesday she recognized the *Greywolds Mercury* lying among the morning newspapers, she looked at its pages with confidence.

She read the *Times* abstractedly, eager to get to the local organ. Her voice lost its intelligent enunciation. Sir Malcolm, with courteous apologies for what might be, he owned, his lack of attention, asked on two occasions for a paragraph to be read over again, the sense of which he had not gathered. Meg, the second time, recognized the implied rebuke, and compelled herself to concentrate her mind upon her task.

When the turn of the *Greywolds Mercury* came she took it up deliberately, and slowly unfolded its pages. She turned to the leader; she glanced over it; the print swam before her eyes. The article was an onslaught upon Sir Malcolm. Last week he had passed a hard sentence upon a poacher caught red-handed in his preserves, and this severity had roused the editor's ire. Meg dropped the paper with an exclamation, her heart beat with indignation and with an exaggerated sense of disappointment.

"What is it, Miss Beecham?" asked Sir Malcolm.

"I cannot read it!" replied Meg unsteadily.

"I suppose it is one of those low-bred, personal attacks upon myself. Pray do not let it discompose you, Miss Beecham," said Sir Malcolm with formal coldness. "I assure you it affects me as little as would the barking of an ill-bred puppy."

As Meg still hesitated he added, after a moment's pause, with impassible politeness, "I must beg you, Miss Beecham, to be so good as to read this article aloud."

The formality of the tone, into which Sir Malcolm had infused a touch of command, reminded Meg that he was her employer, and she proceeded. She went steadily on to the end. The article seemed to her to be marked by increased virulence. She could not judge the merits of the case that formed the subject of the editor's attack. She did not care to judge them. These were outside the point.

The concluding phrases ran: "There is a justice that keeps within the letter of the law, and ignores every suggestion of compassion and fellow-feeling for other human beings. But this justice fails in severity before that which deals out punishment for breaking the edicts contained in the code of so-called social honor. The modern Brutus would immolate not the unhappy peasant only, to whom belong no human rights, he would immolate his own son, if he conspired to rebel against the sacred commandments contained in that code."

Meg was startled by a low exclamation. She looked up. Sir Malcolm was lying back in his chair, his eyes closed, his countenance ashen and drawn.

As she paused he opened his eyes and looked round; his expression was one of mental anguish.

"Thank you," he said, with a ghastly attempt to assume that fine air of dismissal he knew so well how to put on, "that will suffice for to-day."

"May I not do something more for you, sir?" asked Meg, affected by his tone and manner.

"Thank you, I am much obliged," he replied, turning away and taking up a book.

Meg noticed that his hand trembled. She remembered the editor's words. "He was not good to his son."

Was it for this that the reckless allusion to a father's condemnation of a son to death in the name of justice had hit him so hard?

She dared no longer intrude upon the presence of that sorrow or remorse, and left the room. What did it all mean? She went to the great dining-room and stood before the picture with its face turned to the wall. The disgrace appealed to her with tragic piteousness; and the father's unforgiveness acted upon her like a chill repulse.

The house seemed full of an unforgiven pain; the sense of it oppressed Meg, and she wandered out into the amity of the woodland roads. As she walked down a narrow path she became aware of a man approaching toward her from the opposite direction, with a long stride and an absorbed mien. She recognized the editor.

The indignation that had been thrust back by the thought of that unknown sorrow blazed forth anew. It flamed on her cheek and burned in her eyes. As the editor came near he met her glance and removed his hat; but Meg, taking no notice of his salute, passed on, like a little goddess clothed in the panoply of her wrath.

As she returned home by another way she was surprised, and a little offended, to see the editor loitering near the gates of the park. She was preparing to cut him once more, when he advanced resolutely toward her.

"May I say a few words to you, Miss Beecham, with reference to the article that appeared in this morning's *Mercury*?"

"I would prefer not," replied Meg curtly.

"I feel an explanation is due. I would like to justify myself," he said, keeping pace with her as she walked on with her face turned from him.

"I would rather not approach the subject. No explanation is possible," replied Meg coldly.

"I think you are mistaken in saying that. Will you give me the opportunity I ask?"

"I prefer not," repeated Meg, stopping short and now turning round full upon him. "We approach this subject from such totally different standpoints, I feel very seriously about it. You gave your promise lightly, and as lightly broke it. I asked it after much hesitation and reluctance. To address a stranger, to call upon him as I did upon you, was a strong measure to take— a reckless one, some might say. I knew it, I felt it. I put myself into a false position—I exposed myself to the insult of being regarded as one to whom a promise means no bond."

"Not so. That is unjust. Allow me to say you are harsh beyond my deserts," replied the editor, unconsciously raising his voice. Checking himself he resumed more gently: "You will admit that the case of the poacher was entirely different. It was so strong, so startling."

"It was not so much against the matter as against the manner of your attack upon Sir Malcolm Loftdale that I appealed, and that you promised to alter," said Meg, unsoftened.

"I was strongly moved as I wrote," said the editor, who, somewhat to his surprise, found himself pleading before this young girl with eager self-justification. "The severity of the sentence passed upon the unhappy man— I know him and his poor wife—seemed to me so out of all proportion to the offense committed that I forgot everything else. It was only when I looked over the article in print that I realized how the tone of it might hurt you."

"How it might hurt him! It did hurt him! If it is a satisfaction to you to know it, the blow struck home. That allusion to the modern Brutus had its full effect. It went to his heart!" said Meg passionately, with flaming eyes.

"I will not pretend to say, Miss Beecham, except for the apparent neglect of my promise to you, that I would regret the effect of my words upon Sir Malcolm. By his coldness and harshness he drove his son to a piteous death."

"I know nothing of the story to which you allude; and I do not wish to know it. I will not hear it from the lips of an enemy of Sir Malcolm Loftdale," said Meg almost fiercely. "What I do know is, that if it is remorse or sorrow that darkens his old age, it is altogether too sacred a theme to be dragged into print and made the subject of a newspaper attack."

The editor was silent a moment, then he said: "You are right."

The gravity of his tone softened Meg; she hesitated a moment, then inclining her head she moved away.

"I wish you would retract what you said just now concerning your visit to my office," the editor began somewhat blunderingly—"that it was a reckless step—that you consider that it justified me in lightly promising and lightly breaking my pledge."

"You must acknowledge, then, that you forgot all that I said," replied Meg with the childlike bluntness which characterized her.

"Forgive me, and I will never forget again," he replied. "Will you not let me discuss the case of the poacher with you—of the other wrongs that exist— will you help me to advocate the rights of the tenants and laborers without wounding the landlord?"

"I will never discuss with you again," said Meg hastily; and with a quick bow she left him and passed within the gates.

As she went up the avenue she caught sight of Sir Malcolm wandering up and down the yew-tree walk. He saw her and came forward to meet her. The emotion of the morning still left its traces upon his features. He held a letter.

"I have heard from my late secretary," he said. "He writes from London. He will be back in a few days."

"Then, sir, I suppose I must resign my post," said Meg in a pained voice. "I have been happy in serving you."

"You seem to think that all the use you are to me is to serve me, read to me, work for me. Can you conceive yourself of no other use?" said Sir Malcolm in gentler tones than she had ever heard him speak.

"Of what other use can I be, sir, to you?"

"The use of bringing pleasure to me by your simple presence in my house," he said, taking her hand.

"I would be unhappy if I felt myself an idle dependant upon you, sir," Meg said, shy pride giving a touch of awkwardness to her attitude and an embarrassed tone to her voice.

"Were you fond of your task?" he asked.

"I liked it, sir," she replied.

"Then I will write to Mr. Robinson that he may stay where he is. Do not think that I shall be inconsiderate," he went on as she looked up anxiously. "I know that his wish is to find a situation in London. I can get him just the post he desires. Have an easy conscience about him. If you will, indeed, stay to be an old man's eyesight and his right hand, I will be grateful to you. I should be lonely now without you. Will you stay with me, Meg?"

"I will stay with you, sir, till you send me away," said Meg with zeal; and to her surprise she found herself in tears, moved to the heart at the old man's tone of unexpected tenderness.

CHAPTER XXIV.

FRIEND!

From that day a subdued tone of affectionate confidence entered into the relations between Meg and her guardian. Sir Malcolm did not emerge from the seclusion in which he lived so much as from his cold and distant manner. He still took his meals alone, he spent his evenings in solitude, he still wandered alone in the park; but his taciturnity was less marked. He often joined Meg in the grounds, and sometimes they drove out together into the surrounding country.

While continuing to treat her with that dignified courtesy that had a charm for Meg, he assumed toward her a gentle familiarity which kept up a reminder of that unexpected tenderness which had so profoundly moved her on the day when he asked her to stay with him. It was the only time she had seen him relax his stateliness of manner. Meg never knew him to depart from a lofty composure of demeanor. He never gave way to irritability; but if a servant was neglectful of orders, memorable severity visited this breach of duty. Toward her Sir Malcolm assumed a splendid deference. The flowers he plucked for her he presented with a suggestion of the superb homage a regent might give to a child-queen. As he walked and talked with her his conversation showed an appreciation of rustic beauty, and gave evidence of intellectual culture. He told her the names of the trees; he related anecdotes of country life and manners, of illustrious statesmen and persons of note whom he had known; he sometimes flavored his conversation with quotations from the works of classic authors. Sir Malcolm acknowledged, with that fine air which was not one of boasting, still less one of apology, that he knew nothing of contemporary literature outside that of the newspapers—his literary studies terminated with that of the wits of Queen Anne's reign. He spoke with an easy choice of words that gave a balanced elevation to his language. This gentler mood dispelled the fear Meg had felt in his presence, and the fascination grew that he exercised over her. The nobility, the dignity, the sternness of the old man's appearance—the recognition that he was always at his best with her, who was a dependant, added to the spell he exercised over her. The gentle and subtle artificiality—perhaps it were better to say the art—of his manners influenced those of Meg, and they acquired by contact with him an added grace of reserve and composure.

The attacks in the *Mercury* had ceased. Meg attributed Sir Malcolm's brighter mood to their cessation. Week after week elapsed, and the local print, while advocating as forcibly as before the right of the laboring classes to happier conditions brought into their lives, abstained from all personal or covert allusions to Sir Malcolm Loftdale. Meg felt grateful. The editor had done this for her, and the desire grew upon her to thank him.

One afternoon, as she walked about the grounds, she began timidly to draw the baronet's attention to the softened tone of the *Greywolds Mercury*.

Sir Malcolm reared his head, and turning upon her a countenance the features of which seemed to stand out with added definiteness, he said with haughty distinctness: "I have noticed nothing. What an insolent radical thinks fit to say or not to say, matters nothing to me. I utterly ignore it. I regard it as I would regard the advocacy of ruffianism by a member of the criminal classes."

"The attacks pained me," began Meg with regretful hesitation, struggling to master her timidity.

"I know it," replied Sir Malcolm; "and I thank you for your kind heartedness. It was unnecessary pain that you felt. Believe me, the whole affair was unworthy of your consideration. Disdain is the only attitude to assume toward such conduct. No means are too contemptible for a low-born demagogue to adopt for the attainment of his aims."

"But, do you not admit, sir," said Meg with a slight tremor in her deep tones, "that liberalism, if mistaken, yet has its principles?"

"Principles!" repeated Sir Malcolm with scornful clearness. "The burglar, doubtless, has his principles when he picks my lock, and is silent lest he might awake the house. Never mention this man or his paper again."

He left her; and Meg, with a shadow over her face, walked slowly away. She thought there was a certain injustice in not recognizing the altered tone of the newspaper, and the wish came to her more strongly to thank the editor for the deference he had paid to her request.

The next day she was driving out with Sir Malcolm. The way home lay through the straggling market-town, down the High Street, in which stood the office of the *Mercury*. The baronet seldom spoke during a drive, he sat back with that cold and distant air which seemed to withdraw him from his surroundings. The scene impressed itself and made a picture in Meg's mental vision: the red-tiled roofs of the irregular houses coming out against the lemon sky; the office on the southern side of the thoroughfare, the ugly posters glaring in the late sunlight. As they passed the office Meg glanced in its direction; her eyes met those of a man emerging from the doorway. It was the editor. A chill force, that seemed to emanate from the white-haired immobile presence by her side, compelled her to withdraw her eyes and turn them coldly away. It was but for a flash, then Meg looked round to bow and smile her thanks; but the editor had already turned away and was walking with swift, long strides up the street.

Self-upbraidings kept Meg silent during the drive home. The opportunity that she had wished for, of showing to this stranger that she thanked him for his generous fulfillment of the promise he had given to her, had presented itself, and she had used the opportunity to wound him. She sat still and unhappy. In the loneliness of the evening, the pain of having offered what might well be interpreted as an affront by one who had been kind made her restless. A feverish longing came to her to remove the hurt she had given. She thought she would write to this stranger who seemed a friend; but when she endeavored to do so she found the task too difficult. His very name was unknown to her. Allusion to the apparent rudeness of her conduct seemed but to emphasize the incivility she had offered and make explanation inadequate. She put down her pen, and set about thinking once more. She would call upon him and explain! The resolve brought a sense of flurry; but the more she thought over it the more she grew reconciled to it. She owed it to him. She had been to him in anger and to expostulate; she would go to him now in reconciliation and to thank.

The next morning her resolve had not grown the less, but the stronger, for the night's sleep upon it. Meg felt impatient for the hour to come when she could put it into execution. A fretful apprehension was upon her that she would not be able to fulfill her intention. Sir Malcolm proved that day in a mood for relishing her company. With reluctant feet she accompanied him in a ramble through the park. She lent an inattentive ear to his reminiscences in stately English of times long past, of folk who had played their part and were now out of the world's wrangles and reconciliations, its loves, its friendships and estrangements.

Meg was free at last, and with a sense of relief she quickly made her way through the stretching country to the old market town. She did not falter or slacken her pace until she came within sight of the office, then a sudden shyness overcame her. She took some restless steps backward and forward, debating with herself; then the sense that this stranger had been kind to her, that she owed him a debt of gratitude, and that she had inflicted a wound upon him, resumed its ascendency and she went in.

The clerk told her that his master was out. "But I expect him back in five minutes," he added. "Will you walk upstairs, miss?"

Meg was once more shown by her guide into the dingy sanctum. It was as she had seen it before—littered with books, with strips of proof-sheets, and dust. It was imbued with a smell of tobacco. The masculine personality that permeated the room worked upon Meg, and brought on a fit of shyness more overwhelming than the first. Shame at being here came over her, and a longing to escape before the master of the place appeared. She determined to scribble off a few words before he returned.

Writing implements surrounded her on every side. She took up a pen and a sheet of paper. As she drew toward her an ink bottle she knocked something down on the floor. She stooped to pick it up. As she did so a picture hanging in an obscure corner caught her eye. It was in a rude frame. It looked like a colored plate cut out of a fashion-book of some years back. Meg started and drew her breath; a crowd of emotions passed over her. She knew every cluster of roses on that white ball-dress; she knew the affected grace of the simpering figure's posture; she remembered that mended tear right across the page. As she looked at it the room in which she sat became full of the hubbub of a London street. It was a room similar to this one—littered with books and paper, imbued with the smell of tobacco; in it sat a young man with kind bright eyes, and a mane of blond hair; he was carefully pasting that inane representation of a lady, and by his side a child, neglected and forlorn, stood eagerly watching the strong hands as they repaired the beloved print.

A mist gathered before Meg's eyes. This child in the shabby frock was herself; this battered and mended fashion-plate was the idolized imaginary picture of her mother. That young man with the kind eyes and the deft fingers, who was he?

Meg was still gazing at the conventional figure in the ball-dress when the door opened, and the editor walked in.

She vaguely recognized that his demeanor was altered. He bowed distantly.

MEG RECOGNIZES THE OLD FASHION-PLATE.—Page 284.

"I came to thank you and to explain," began Meg, and paused. Memory had touched her eyelids and she recognized him. The puzzling recollection that had obtruded itself with vague pertinacity asserted itself triumphantly. She knew now why she had thought of this stranger as a friend.

"To explain?" he repeated; and he, too, paused.

"Yes; about yesterday. I saw you," she said abruptly, almost mechanically, as if speaking by rote and eager to get done; "but I was afraid to bow to you, because I was with Sir Malcolm Loftdale. It was mean and weak of me when I owe you so much."

"You owe me nothing. You convinced me, and I acted upon my new conviction," he answered, still in a distant tone.

"I have much to be thankful to you for," she repeated in a voice that was hoarse with emotion. "Where did you get this?" she added brusquely, interrupting herself and pointing to the fashion-plate.

He looked surprised and said:

"I have had it some years."

"Who gave it to you?" she asked.

He looked curiously at her. "A story is attached to that picture," he answered evasively.

"Is your name William Standish?" she asked.

"Yes," he replied. "Did you not know my name was Standish?" he added, puzzled by the expression of her face.

She shook her head in denial. "Was it a child gave you this picture?"

"Yes," he replied, monosyllabic in his surprise.

"To her foolish, lonely fancy was it the portrait of her mother, who had died in giving her birth?"

"That is true," he replied. Then he added earnestly, "Do you know anything of that child? Can you tell me anything about her? I have tried to find her. I have made many efforts to do so, but in vain. I have lost all clew to her."

"Was her name Meg?" she asked.

"Yes, her name was Meg—dear little Meg!" he said, his eyes shining softly, as if he were seeing before him an image that delighted him.

"I am, or rather I was little Meg," she said in a low voice.

"You?" he exclaimed, looking at her.

She nodded.

"But I thought your name was Beecham," he said. "That of Meg, I understood, was Browne."

"Till I went to school I believed my name was Browne; but one day I was told it was Beecham," she said.

"You Meg, little Meg!" he replied, his eyes traveling slowly over her. "I can scarcely believe it."

"But all the same it is I!" she said with a laugh, as he kept looking at her. "Let me prove my identity—put me to the test; you will see how correctly I will answer," she said. "I remember the night when you put that patch on the old fashion-plate. I had crumpled it up in despair because you said that probably my mother was not a lady."

"That is true!" he replied, still looking scrutinizingly at her.

"I remember how I used to tease you about your dinners. I was quite motherly with you!"

"Motherly! Grandmotherly! Bless you, little Meg!" he cried, and then he laughed. "Is it you? Is it really you?" and he stretched out his two hands.

Meg placed hers into their clasp. "Yes, it is little Meg for whom you did that kind thing, of stopping the attacks upon Sir Malcolm."

"That was for tall Meg!" he said.

"Tall Meg, who I fear, did what little Meg would never have done: appearing to ignore a kindness out of fear."

"No, no, we will not talk of that. It was so natural," he said, still looking at her with surprised and friendly eyes.

They fell to chat, interchanging memories of those old childish days. He walked with her across the country to the gates of the park, and as they walked still they chatted of that fond, silly past.

CHAPTER XXV.

FOR "AULD LANG SYNE."

Although Meg could not explain to herself the right of authority Sir Malcolm had over her, she felt it and acknowledged his control. The temptation often came to enjoy the society of the friend of her childhood, but her honest nature shrank from meeting him secretly; and yet the attacks on the old baronet that had appeared in the local paper precluded the possibility of mentioning to him its editor's name.

Still she longed to see Mr. Standish. One day she thought she would venture to ask Sir Malcolm's permission. She began, blundering a little about the debt of gratitude which she owed to him, and which it was her pleasure to acknowledge; his wishes, she said, would ever influence her in her acts and her conduct. Then, with a blush, she admitted there was something she wished to do, for which she wished to get his permission. Meg was amazed at the manner in which the old gentleman met her advances. He distinctly disclaimed any shadow of authority over her.

"But you have been so good to me, sir," she replied. "But for you, when I ran away from school———"

"When you ran away from school," he interrupted with unexpected coldness. "I was almost inclined, when you refused to enter the carriage, to leave you on the road. If I have given you protection it is for reasons I do not care to explain. I have told you, I do not want gratitude. The tie between us is a voluntary one. You are free as air, young lady, but always with a risk. Your acts will not be disobediences, though they may be imprudences. Distinctly remember you are your own mistress. Keep your secrets if you have any. I do not demand your confidence."

"Free as air!" rang through Meg's heart. "I am my own mistress; free to meet my friend again."

After this extraordinary ebullition of candor from Sir Malcolm, the old gentleman's kindness seemed to regain its late level. Meg even fancied that he was kinder, as if he endeavored thus to salve any wound to her feelings which his temporary harshness might have occasioned.

Still he had said she was free as air, and Meg now felt justified in acting as her heart impelled her. The winter came and went, but it brought no sense of dreariness or bleakness to Meg. She had found the friend of her childhood, and the reflection of her childhood's days shone over everything. It was no wonder that she felt some of the charm of the old companionship with him who had been good to her when all the world had neglected her; and the memory of whose kindness had set a halo about the memory of her forlorn life.

She asked herself no questions concerning the nature of this new interest; she knew only that until it came back to her she was as one walled in, and without daylight. The real Meg had lived captive in a state of repression; to no one had she ventured to tell her impressions; but to this friend she could speak of the most trivial event, and confide the most intimate thought. He drew her out with a frank tenderness that won her simple trust. There grew a fascination to walk and to talk with him; to tell him all that had happened to her since the day of their parting. She had never forgotten him; the thought of him had ever dwelt in her mind, ready to start up and welcome him at his coming. And although it was still her pleasure and her duty to minister to her benefactor's need, yet by his own injunction she felt herself free to yield to the refreshment and delight of those meetings.

They met at sunset, after the journalist's work was done, in the wood behind the house; and their trysting-place was an elm.

"It looks like an old wizard," said Mr. Standish, pointing to the leafless tree standing gaunt against the dying light.

"Old Merlin!" said Meg; "and there is the eerie brightness about him. He is going to throw a spell over us."

The prediction proved true; a spell was cast about Meg's life, and she loved no spot on earth as she loved the place by that tree.

No young girl ever set forth to her first ball with more expectation and longing than did Meg feel in anticipation of some new chat with the lost friend whom she had found again. Endless, endless appeared to her the sources of interesting conversation and of sentiment that he had at his command, and each time they met and talked it seemed to her that he opened a new world of thought and imagination for her spirit to dwell in.

They had a thousand subjects to speak about. Every topic came at random. They cared not which it was, for each seemed ever new. Meg was like a child who has never seen the sea, now picking up rainbow shells by the shore; every shell different in the heap lying beside her in a glorious chance medley.

Sometimes he entertained her with scenes of travel, of striving and success. Sometimes they interchanged memories, mutually reminding each other of incidents in the past. With grave humor, followed by hearty laughter, he would describe the part she had played in some scene where she had behaved with great motherliness and dignity toward him. He would tell her how she had never despaired of him, although the bailiffs were after him.

"But I was a sad trouble to you, Meg," he vowed. "You were a little tyrant then. Where is all that tyranny gone?"

"You give me no excuse to exercise it," she replied one day. "The instinct may be there still; but you are so good, so absorbed in work now."

"Ah, if you only knew it!" he exclaimed. "Little Meg would have been more quick-sighted. She would have sternly reproved me, and preached to me about wasting my time when I should be furnishing copy."

"Copy! What is copy?" she asked.

"Blessed ignorance! Copy is that which goes to fill those columns of print. It is what the hungry printer clamors for, and looks very black when he does not get."

Meg laughed.

"You speak as if printers were wild beasts fed with leaders on schemes for extending the franchise or removing some dowdy old tax."

"Well, well, I am a humbug. All the time that I am writing these leaders I am thinking of coming to see you; I hurry through my work in order to be in time to meet you, Meg," he answered.

"Then I will meet you no more if I spoil your work," she said gravely.

"There spoke the child. All the severity of the little monitor of yore is in those accents," he replied with a laugh. "No, Meg, I work all the better to earn my play."

"Your play?" she said slowly, with a slight emphasis on the word; and she was silent awhile. The expression remained with her, casting its little shadow of doubt, and she would harp back upon it.

"Is this your play?" she would question gravely, when he said anything complimentary.

They had their merry wrangles, their desperate fallings-out, their pretty makings-up. Meg, with characteristic repartees, parried his thrusts, and their intercourse was sweet with wholesome laughter. With a blunt playfulness she met anything approaching to sentiment.

"While I was waiting," he said one day, "there was a little bird up there— you'll hear it—which continually says, 'She'll come! she'll come!'"

"And I heard a cuckoo in the wood as I came along," she replied; "he cried nothing but 'Copy! copy! copy!'"

"It must have been the printer's devil," he said, "when I was taking a holiday."

An innocent coquetry, which was the simple outcome of delight in her ever-growing happiness, would tinge her manner with a little salt of aggressiveness. She sometimes played at making him jealous.

She was late one day; she had been detained, she explained, by a fascinating being.

"Who was he?"

She would not tell his name, but vowed he had splendid lustrous eyes, and a mustache an officer in the guards might envy.

Mr. Standish laughed, and seemed inclined to turn the conversation to another topic.

"You do not ask his name," she said; "yet this fascinating creature made me late, and with difficulty I tore myself from his spell."

"But you came," he replied, falling into her mood.

"My sense of duty. I am naturally punctual. I push it to a weakness."

"I wish to forget him," he said; "he has robbed me enough. What is the name of the country bumpkin?"

"Country bumpkin, indeed! He wears a coat the fit of which the most fashionable tailor might well envy the secret of its cut—a coat black and glossy, with just a touch of white at the throat."

"The rector. I knew it. Confess it is the rector," Mr. Standish said with finger uplifted.

"No white-haired rector, indeed," said Meg.

"Then the curate? All the ladies are fascinated by the curate."

"Not the curate. My charmer is an inmate of the house."

"An inmate?" repeated Mr. Standish, perplexed.

"On the day of my arrival he was so pleasant and cordial his greeting almost made me feel at home."

"I wonder who he is!" said Mr. Standish.

"As you look troubled, I will be generous and tell you," said Meg, and paused.

"Well," said Mr. Standish, "who is he?"

"My charmer of the admirable coat, the impressive mustache, and the splendid eyes is—well—my black cat. He it was who received me cordially, sat by my fire, purred a welcome, and followed me about with a tail straight as that;" and she lifted her parasol to a perpendicular.

Sometimes the talk drifted to Sir Malcolm's son, who had been the editor's friend, and whose portrait, turned to the wall, appealed with a piteous interest to Meg, and was always recurring to her mind.

"He had many faults," Mr. Standish admitted one day. "He was reckless, but there was a winsomeness about him that won hearts; and the fault he committed which rankled deepest in the old baronet's mind was an action that came nearer to a virtue."

"What was that fault?" she asked.

"He married the woman he loved. She was the prettiest, sweetest woman I ever saw. Absurd as it may seem, Meg, the first time I saw you grown up you reminded me of her. It was simply fancy, of course the likeness is lost now. It seems to have gone out."

"Do you think it was because of this marriage that his portrait was turned to the wall?" persisted Meg.

"I think so. At least this I know: Sir Malcolm never forgave that marriage."

"But why?" asked Meg.

"Because she was poor and brave enough to work for her living. I believe she was a governess; but her trials came after their marriage. His debts accumulated, his father was unforgiving; he sometimes had to hide."

"What became of her?" still questioned Meg.

"She died when her child was born. After her death he certainly grew more reckless. He was unhappy, and I think he had some remorse. The marriage took place on the continent."

"Did the child live?"

"I don't know. He certainly had no home for it. He never alluded to it. I believe he was not with his wife when she died."

"Poor wife!" said Meg, thinking of that unhappy wife who had suffered so much, who had died so neglected and uncared for. "Is it not strange," she continued after a pause, "that it should have been my guardian's son who was the friend for whom you almost beggared yourself?"

"And for having done which, do you remember, you stroked my head?" he replied smilingly.

She answered him with a blush only.

Sometimes he spoke to her as to a comrade out of the fund of his large experience and knowledge. His interest in the working classes appealed to her, and life seemed to grow wider from the solicitude that he brought into it for others. There grew every day in her heart a reliance, a sort of wide faith in him, as if all he said and thought must be right.

The winter passed and the spring came round; the sap rose in the earth and the pulses of nature quickened.

They met oftener. Sometimes they wandered forth to meet each other in the dewy mornings, when the fields shone like gossamer. There, in the woods, where the birds wearied themselves for listeners, they came on the scene. Meg would bid him forget his politics, his ink-bottle, in honor of all the loveliness around.

"Look at this clump of daffodils," she said one morning when a mood of mirthful raillery was upon her, pointing to the silly flowers. "Don't they look like Hebes drooping their gold cups? Ah! everything is young and merry, sir, but your old politics—your dull old politics."

Then he vowed he would never talk politics to her again, upon which she coaxed and played the little siren until he relented, complaining that she honeycombed his will by her cajoleries.

An exaltation stirred Meg's spirit—the girl who had been silent and reserved was full of innocent gayety; and still that companionship with one who had brought happiness to her childhood continued simple, familiar, and charming, as it might be between dearest friends.

Sir Malcolm had an attack of illness, and as Meg devoted herself to him for some time there were no meetings at the elm. Then she became conscious of the value of the enchantment this new-found relationship brought into her life; and when they met again she was aware of a subtle change in the sentiment with which she regarded the relations between Mr. Standish and herself.

While compelling herself to greet him with the same equable friendliness, she was often chilled by the awkwardness of self-restraint. The facile word lagged when she tried to assume an attitude of bantering reserve, and her sincere nature oftener hid itself behind that of shy formality. She would then gravely inquire of his work, awkwardly plunge into politics or surface topics, but after awhile in his reassuring presence the pain of her embarrassed spirit would vanish, and she would feel comforted. In the sweetness of restored harmony between them, after the jar of repression, her heart would expand, and again she would weave around him a web of delicate sympathy and winsome pleasantry. She would be a child again, and would display her old quickness of mood to suit his disposition—gay when he wished to be gay, serious when he was serious, silent when he was inclined for silence. In this childlike docility and wistful eagerness to please him dwelt the old wakeful and sensitive pride, quick to take alarm, easily perplexed. The happy confidence would take flight like a frightened bird, the laughter of her heart would be quenched, the trustful approaches of her spirit checked as quickly as had been those of the susceptible child, so coy and yet so devoted.

One day he did not come. In the evening she received a note of explanation. He had been detained by business; he had come too late, and he had waited, hoping some kindly inspiration would lead her to see if he had kept tryst after the appointed hour. But she had not come. Would she be gracious and come the next day?

After a debate with herself Meg sallied forth. Again he was not there, and a dull, unhappy anger took possession of her. She was returning at once, but a shower came. She stood under a tree waiting for it to pass, but the trailing cloud seemed never to empty. She was angry, and she felt about to cry for being imprisoned there. The raindrops began to saturate the tree. She would not forgive him; twice to have failed her! She had her upbraiding of him so perfect by going over it, she wished he might come in time to deliver it. She heard steps approaching, and she kept her eyes sternly before her. It was only a countrywoman with sloppy shoes. Her heart went down, and tears rushed to her eyes; and so full was she of her grievance that when he joined her with the rain streaming from his hat she started, not having heard him come, and all her prepared reproaches left her memory. She did not give him her hand, however, and tried to flick away the telltale tears.

"I am late again. I am so sorry. I could not help it," he said earnestly.

"But I can help coming in future," said Meg in a severe tone.

"No, you could not punish me like this," he said. "It was a telegram from London upon which I was obliged to write a short article which kept me. That article was written in such desperation that I shall be afraid to read it in print. Won't you give me your hand?"

"The shower is over. I think I shall go back," she said.

"Do you see that black cloud shaped like an Inverness cape? It is coming right up with its deluge."

"All the more reason that I should hurry home," she said.

"But consider, Meg," he replied, smiling down upon her; "what an undignified retreat. Before you have gone a hundred yards you will be obliged to break into a run, and finally make another stage under yonder elm tree, where I will rejoin you; and then we will begin all over again. Nothing like a good rainstorm for a reconciliation. But all the grace of it is gone. Come now, I have felt the first menacing drop upon my nose. Make friends, it says."

She looked at him with scrutinizing gravity, then a smile broke.

"I cannot resist the drop's appeal," she replied with a laugh, and she put out her hand. "Still, for all the rain in the world," she continued, "I must air my grievance. I had a good right to be angry. I waited nearly twenty minutes yesterday."

"I waited two hours," he replied.

"But you came at a wrong hour," she said. "I came at the hour you appointed. Look at this—just look at this, and you will be silent."

She took out his note, opened it, and held it under his eyes.

"I know—I know," he said; "that perjured note. But all is forgiven now."

The cape of cloud passed away, and the sun came out.

There was a good-humored strength about Mr. Standish that puzzled Meg, and she often longed to pierce the mystery—at least the mystery to her—of his nature. But after a time his manner changed; a melancholy grew upon him. One day he turned and said: "You call me your friend, Meg. You keep dwelling on the memories of those fond silly days of your childhood. But you are a child no longer. Perhaps we had better think of one another, and cease those happy walks."

"Cease those walks!" she exclaimed with a gasp in her voice. He remained silent. Then she said proudly: "If you think so, really—" but her voice failed, and with a sudden cry she exclaimed, "I knew it could not last—that you must tire of me."

"Tire of you, Meg!" he cried, facing round upon her. "It is because I love you that I say this. But it is not as the friend of your childhood that I love you. We must make no mistake. I love you as the man loves the one woman in all the world he wants for his wife. If you cannot accept that love from me I would prefer not to see you again."

She did not reply, and she averted her face. When she looked slowly up, even in the tension of waiting for her answer, he felt something of the thrill he might have experienced if a spirit had answered to his call. The child he had known was looking back at him. A something he had missed—a mystery of spiritual identity with the Meg of long ago, glimmerings of which he had caught—had waked up. It was the child grown to be a woman—endowed with a woman's soul, gifted with a thousandfold powers of feeling. She did not speak; her silence, her quivering features, her kindling countenance answered him.

"Meg!" he said in a low voice, and bending forward he drew her to him.

CHAPTER XXVI.

BEFORE THE PICTURE.

Meg delayed announcing the news of her engagement to Sir Malcolm. She feared the effect upon him of hearing that she had betrothed herself to the man who had written those attacks in the local newspaper. Sir Malcolm had been ailing during the winter.

"She could not leave him yet," she told her lover. "It was her duty to remain with him." And he agreed that it was for awhile.

The crisis, however, came sooner than she anticipated. A trouble had been fermenting in Sir Malcolm's secret thoughts. He had noticed Meg's absences. Always regular at her post at the hours when he required her services as secretary and reader, he missed her companionship in his walks; he had lost the certainty of meeting her in the drawing-room, in her little study with her books, or at the piano.

One morning, on returning from her tryst in the woods, she met the baronet at the gates of the park. "You are out early, Miss Beecham," he said with constrained courtesy.

"I hope, sir, I am not late," she replied anxiously.

"You are always punctual—a model of punctuality—in the discharge of your duties. It is scarcely half-past ten," he replied in a ceremonious tone, with the slightest emphasis on the word duties. As they walked toward the house he added, "Far be it from me to imply that I have a right to claim more of the pleasure of your society than you care to give me."

"I am afraid, sir, you have missed me—" she began.

"I have told you I am a solitary; I miss no one," he interrupted with that directness of speech which might have been brutal, had it not been veiled by the art he possessed of lofty politeness.

"There is something I want to tell you, sir, that I ought to have told you before," began Meg, her heart beating and her cheeks flushing, as she felt that the hour of revelation had come.

The baronet's gaze rested upon her with an illconcealed flicker of anxiety. But he said in his finest manner that he would be happy to listen to anything she had to say; but perhaps the interview had best be deferred until they reached his study.

When they came there Meg began hesitatingly: "The post that I have filled, sir, in your household has been one of pleasure to me; still what is difficult to say I must say now—I must resign it."

"Resign it!" exclaimed Sir Malcolm, bending his eyes upon her. "For what reason?"

"I have formed an attachment, sir. I am engaged to be married," she replied with the calmness of fright.

"Married!" ejaculated Sir Malcolm. "Engaged without having consulted me! Nonsense; you mean to tell me—" He paused. "But this is monstrous." He got up, walked up and down the room. Meg watched him in silence, astonished at what seemed to her an extraordinary outburst of emotion. After a few moments Sir Malcolm regained his composure, and sitting down again said in a constrained, business-like tone, "You will admit that, at least, as your guardian, I should have been told of this before. To whom are you engaged?"

She hesitated under the influence of a gaze, the keenness of which stopped confidence at its source.

"To one who was very good to me in my childhood. When no one else cared for me he was my only friend."

"Have you corresponded with him ever since your childhood?"

"No, sir; I met him here. I had lost sight of him for years."

"Is he of low birth?" asked the baronet with frigid brusqueness.

"No, sir. But if he were—" She paused and looked at the old man with a glance steady as his own.

"I understand. You assert your right to marry who you will—clodhopper or landowner. Perhaps, however, you will admit, as I observed just now, that as your guardian I am justified in asking questions about this young man?"

"I gladly admit it, sir, and thank you; for it is another proof of the interest—the generous interest—you have lavished upon me," she said warmly.

"May I ask to what profession he belongs?" demanded Sir Malcolm.

"He is a writer," said Meg, and paused.

"A writer? That is somewhat vague," said Sir Malcolm.

"A journalist," she resumed, and again she paused.

Sir Malcolm knit his brows.

"It is difficult for me to explain," continued Meg, raising her eyes and speaking low, but quite firmly. "The circumstances that led to our meeting were so strange—in a manner they are painful. They may place me in a false light—I may appear ungrateful. The friend of my childhood is Mr. Standish, the editor of the *Greywolds Mercury*."

"Of the paper that dragged my name into print and held it up to public ignominy in its columns?" observed Sir Malcolm.

Meg bowed her head, and said falteringly: "These articles led to our meeting. I had called at the office to remonstrate, to expostulate with the writer."

"To expostulate, to remonstrate!" cried Sir Malcolm with a burst of outraged pride. "What! You exposed me to this humiliation; you begged quarter for me of this insolent radical. It was a grievous injury you did me!" He checked himself, then resumed with deliberate calm: "But let that pass. It is your marriage with this man we were discussing. I forbid it; I cannot countenance such an engagement."

"I think, sir," said Meg after a pause, speaking steadily, but in a feeling voice, "that after reflection you will admit that you are claiming too much authority over me. Mr. Standish and I love each other, and we admit the right of no third person to part us. I know you have been my secret benefactor for a long time; yet it is more than a benefactor's due you are claiming. A father only would have the right to impose the authority over me you demand to establish."

"It is this authority over you that I demand and that I rightly possess," said the baronet in a weighty voice, rising and drawing himself up. "You are my only son's only child. I stand in your father's place toward you. I am your grandfather."

"My grandfather!" said Meg stupidly. Everything grew indistinct around her except the figure of the old man, standing erect, authoritative, the sun shining on his white hair, illumining it like a halo round his head.

"Follow me!" he said. He turned and she followed automatically. He preceded her down the great staircase. The perfume of flowers came to her dreamily. Still she followed her guide on and on—vaguely conscious that some great issue was at hand.

They entered the large dining-room. Sir Malcolm had signed to two servants in the hall to follow.

They walked straight to where the picture hung with its face turned to the wall, an outcast among that goodly painted company.

At the order of the master the picture was turned, and the servants left the room. "That is your father's portrait," said Sir Malcolm in a voice that sounded without a quaver.

She knew that he turned away and left her standing there, looking at the representation of a young man dressed in a scarlet and gold uniform. He had a gallant and winsome air, his features were femininely delicate, the blue, small eyes bright, the lips full. As a sudden realization that she was looking at her father's face came to her, a tumult of feeling swept over Meg. Then came a chill and a disappointment. The countenance said nothing to her; she gazed at it dry-eyed.

She moved away. Sir Malcolm's glance was steadily averted. As she approached he looked round. His features were tense with suppressed emotion; a flicker of wildness lit the eyes, lustrous with unshed tears.

"It is a beautiful face," said Meg softly, moved by the evidences of a mental struggle that gave a crazy look of anguish to the old face; "but it is not dear to me, sir, as yours is dear."

"It does not do him justice; he was the handsomest lad in the country," said the old man. "I loved him, Meg; I staked all my pride in life upon him. When he disgraced me my pride in life left me."

"Ah! how could he bring this sorrow upon you, sir?" murmured Meg, scarce knowing what she said, confused by this outburst of confidence from one whom she had always known so reticent.

"He brought dishonor upon our name," said the old man. Meg saw that he flushed and that he trembled; but he went on quietly nevertheless. "I must explain to you now why this picture was turned to the wall. I must tell you— what is agonizing to me to tell, and must be painful to you to hear; but the circumstances compel me. He wronged you. I have tried to fill his place toward you. He married your mother abroad, and under a false name. He contracted debts—debts of honor—that, having the money, he yet never paid. Thank God! the extent of his dishonor was never made public." Sir Malcolm paused, then he resumed: "His last act was, perhaps, the redeeming feature of his life. He killed himself. His suicide showed that a gleam of the old spirit made a dishonored life unbearable to him."

Meg did not speak. The horror of that tragedy filled the room. After a silence the old man resumed in his more habitual manner and tone:

"We need never refer to this unhappy story again. Ask me nothing concerning your mother; I never saw her, and know next to nothing about her. She died in giving you birth." Again he paused, then slowly with effort he said: "Will you forgive me, Meg, for your neglected childhood?"

Meg made a deprecatory gesture, and uttered an exclamation. These words of entreaty from him hurt her like a blow.

"I ask you to forgive it," continued the baronet with emotion. "I humbly ask it from my soul. I have remorse for it. I admit that in your childhood I looked upon you with aversion—that your coming here was a pain to me; and yet I loved you before you came."

"Before I came?" murmured Meg, astonished.

"I have loved you ever since the day I brought you back to school. When I saw you so spent with anguish and fatigue, lying on the cushions before me, my heart went out to you. I stopped my carriage when I was driving off after having left you; I returned, I came to your little bedside and kissed you in the dark."

"Then it was you who gave me that kiss!" faltered Meg. "I have never forgotten it." And on the impulse she pressed her lips on his thin hand.

"You have made me love you—you have wound yourself round my heart. Forgive me, Meg," said the old man.

"Do not ask me to forgive you, sir. I have received nothing but good from you," said Meg.

"Say it, Meg," the old man urged. "Say, 'Grandfather, I forgive it and forget it.'"

"As you wish I will say it, sir. I forgive—" began Meg.

"Say, 'Grandfather,'" he interrupted.

"Grandfather, I forgive it and forget it," repeated Meg, stretching out her hands.

He took them then, looking down into her eyes. "Can you, forgetting the part I played of neglect, forget also the part of kindness played in it by that man? For my sake can you forget it?"

The words struck the chords of Meg's heart and filled it with the memory of the love that had come to her in her forlornness, and that now filled her life with all youth's appeals.

"No, sir, I can never forget that—never!" she said, loosening her hands from his grasp and stepping away.

"If you persist in this engagement, I will not disguise it from you, Meg, you will strike the last prop from under me—it will break my heart!" said Sir Malcolm.

The words crushed once more the rising mutiny in Meg's heart. The tyranny of pity mastered its revolt—insisted upon the new duty to the new loyalty.

She moved away restlessly; then suddenly throwing her arms up with a gesture of despair she sank into a chair, and hiding her face in her hands she burst into tears.

The old man waited until her sobs grew quieter; then he said:

"Come with me, Meg; we will go to Mr. Standish together."

CHAPTER XXVII.

IN THE EDITOR'S OFFICE.

A few moments later Meg was walking by her grandfather's side. He had refused to drive. Sir Malcolm never said a word, but he seemed in hot haste. Meg's thoughts were in a tumult. What was he going to do? How would he meet his former enemy? Had he been softened?

The old baronet gripped his stick as he went along and planted it firmly on the road. She would have given anything to have questioned him; but fear on the one hand lest she should exasperate him, on the other a failing heart lest if he were inclined to conciliation she might balk the impulse by some well-meant blunder kept her silent.

When they reached the office, and her grandfather asked the clerk if Mr. Standish was at home, she tried to judge his mood by the tone of his voice. For an instant she hoped the clerk's answer would be in the negative; but the young man, leaving his desk, replied that Mr. Standish was at home, adding with an air of bewilderment: "Sir Malcolm Loftdale, I believe?"

"Take my card up," said the baronet, pulling out his cardcase.

They climbed up the narrow stairs, and Meg saw her lover standing by his table to receive them. With a bow as cold, Mr. Standish returned the old gentleman's frigid salutation. He was stretching out his hand to her, but with a little anxious frown she signaled to him to take no notice of her at present.

"You are, I believe, sir, the responsible editor of the *Greywolds Mercury*," said the baronet with a chill civility that brought a sorrowful anticipation to Meg.

Mr. Standish in a constrained voice acknowledged his position. "I am afraid that this places me in an unfavorable light before you, sir," he continued in a half-apologetic tone.

Sir Malcolm moved his hand. "You mistake the object of my visit if you think, sir, that I ask for an explanation—if you suppose that articles upon myself which appeared some months ago, and which no doubt had literary merit, have produced upon me the slightest impression. I am ready to admit the right of every man to his opinions. I have my own opinions on a subject which I would prefer not to express."

He paused, and Mr. Standish remained silent, waiting for his visitor to continue.

"My motive for entering a publishing office," the baronet went on, looking round him with a cold smile, "is from a widely different motive. I will refer to one of those articles only for the simple sake of illustration. You were very indignant, sir, at my stringent suppression of a poacher. Now, sir, I beg you in justice to give me your opinion of a poacher in a moral sense—one who, by assignations, by means at his command, contrives to inveigle the affections of a young girl, almost a child, intruding himself thus dishonestly into a gentleman's family."

"Sir Malcolm Loftdale," said Mr. Standish firmly yet courteously, "I perfectly understand your meaning. This young lady occupies an honorable position in your household, and she has always led me to understand that you treated her with the utmost kindness and consideration; but she is not a member of your family."

"Such being your impression, I will not presume to blame you," said the baronet with the cynical courtesy one uses to an inferior. "Your honorable intentions I take for granted. It only remains for me to inform you, in the presence of this young lady—who has herself been made acquainted by me within the hour of the position she holds in my house—that Miss Beecham is my granddaughter."

"Your granddaughter!" repeated Mr. Standish with a movement of surprise. "I thought, sir, you had but one child—a son?"

"She is the daughter and only child of that son," answered the baronet with lofty curtness. "There is no necessity for me to enter with you into the details of a family history. Suffice it to say that I beg of you, as an honorable literary man"—the old gentleman laid a slight sarcastic stress on the word literary— "never again to address this lady, and to terminate from this moment an acquaintance which, if pursued, must be henceforth termed clandestine, treacherous, and dishonorable."

At these words Mr. Standish drew himself up with a dignity as cold and stern as was that of his visitor. "Sir Malcolm Loftdale," he said, "this comes rather late. It is not for me to give the pledge you exact; I will give it at the request of Miss Beecham only."

For a moment irritation seemed about to surprise the old gentleman. He clinched his stick and reared his grand old head as for a rebuke; then he turned mutely toward Meg.

"You have applied the word dishonorable to me, Sir Malcolm Loftdale. Allow me to say it is the last word, I think, you should have employed," resumed Mr. Standish.

"Sir, your protestations are thrown away upon me. I have no more to say to you," replied the baronet. "Meg, my child, it is now for you to decide. You have heard the expression of my positive wishes; you know how I feel on this subject; you know better than any one how your decision one way or the other will affect me. I confide in you."

Meg wrung her hands and remained silent. In her despair she confusedly felt she was called upon to make her choice between two duties. One was heavy to follow, the other meant all the happiness of her young heart. She gave an inarticulate moan—a word of that primal language common to all creation in its moments of anguish.

"I do not ask you to speak," said Sir Malcolm. "Put your hand on my arm, Meg, and let me take you home—that will suffice."

"I cannot—I cannot!" she moaned, moving a few irresolute steps away from the two between whom her fate lay. She could not speak the word that must bring sorrow to one who was weak, lonely, and already heavily stricken, still less that other word which must crush the young, the strong, and the beloved one.

"Before you ask this young lady to retract," she heard the voice of her lover say; then he paused as if to change the phrase to one more generously worded: "Before you ask her to refuse me for your sake, will you grant me a few moments' private conversation?"

"No, sir," answered the baronet. "I repeat I have said all I have to say to you. I wish this interview to end. Come back with me, Meg."

"You have addressed me as one capable of dishonorable conduct," Mr. Standish resumed quietly. "This young lady's father, sir, if he were alive, would have been the last to apply such a term to me."

"Her father! What do you know of her father?" said Sir Malcolm savagely.

"If Philip Loftdale was her father, I knew him well. He often called me his dearest friend."

Meg, leaning back against the wall, saw her grandfather staring vacantly at the speaker. "What do you mean? Who are you, sir?" he asked.

"Again I ask you, sir," said Mr. Standish with sudden gentleness, "for a few moments' private conversation."

"No, sir; if you have anything to say, speak out before this young lady. I took the step of leading Miss Beecham here that she might judge the merits of the case for herself. I am sorry to have to add that the assertion you have just made, that you were my son's friend, is no recommendation to me. He was unfortunate in his associates."

Mr. Standish did not reply. He took out a bunch of keys and fitted one into a drawer. Meg saw him draw out a bundle of letters. He kept his eyes averted from her as he said:

"I shrink from telling the particulars I must now state, or of hinting at an obligation. But I am playing for a great stake—one that is all the world to me; and I see no means of moving you, sir, but by referring to this fact, and bringing evidences of its truth before you."

He laid his hand upon the letters.

"It is your wish, sir, that I should speak before Miss Beecham. Perhaps it is as well that she should hear what I have to say."

"It is my wish. Go on, sir!" said Sir Malcolm fiercely as Mr. Standish paused.

"Your son was adjutant of his regiment. Whatever were his follies and recklessness, he was a good soldier. He was trusted by his comrades, and he was proud of their trust. You were stern with him, sir—I shall not say overstern. It is not for me to judge."

"Go on, sir," said the old man.

"Since his marriage, if you remember, you held no communication with him——"

"If your claim upon me," interrupted the baronet fiercely, "is that you are a relation of the unhappy woman he married, I think you must admit that the fact that I have recognized her daughter, and that I mean publicly to declare her my grandchild, is a reparation which answers all claims and silences all appeals."

"I make no claim upon you. I think I will establish that I am no—" Mr. Standish paused, then resumed: "If you remember, your son wrote to you shortly before his death a letter that you returned unopened, as you had done others before."

Sir Malcolm did not reply, and for a moment there was a dead silence. Mr. Standish resumed with difficulty:

"That letter, sir, was to ask you for three hundred pounds, that in a reckless moment he had taken from the money belonging to his regiment, convinced that he would be able to repay it."

Still the old man remained silent as death, looking with a fixed gaze upon the speaker.

"Your son came to me. Dishonor faced him. He told me of his folly. The next day he would be disgraced if he failed to raise the money."

Sir Malcolm drew a heavy breath; he parted his lips as if to speak, but no words came; and he listened intently.

"God knows, sir," resumed the young man, "that I tell you what follows with the utmost unwillingness. I had the money he needed so sorely, and I let him have it. His honor was saved. His act remained unknown to his brother-officers and to the world, but he felt the stigma too bitterly to live."

The old man sat down and took the proffered documents. He read them through hurriedly, and Meg noticed that once he brushed away a tear. Then he rose, and with a large and liberal action put out a trembling hand to the editor, who clasped it in his.

"Mr. Standish," said the baronet, "you have saved what is dearer to me than life—my family honor. I will do, sir, what I have never done before. I ask your pardon. I acknowledge an obligation to you that I can never repay."

"You can repay it, grandfather," said Meg through tears.

"You can repay it, sir—ay, and brimming over," said Mr. Standish. "The stake I have played for, as I said, is all the world to me. I love this lady with a love that can never change. I loved her as a child, I love her as a girl, I will love her as a woman all her life. Do not part us!"

"Grandfather, do not part us!" repeated Meg in a voice hoarse with pleading. "I will never desert you!"

The old gentleman hesitated. He resumed his seat, and putting his elbow on the table he covered his eyes with his hand. There was anxious silence in the room. At last Sir Malcolm rose, and with a grave dignity he went to Meg, and taking her hand he placed it in that of her lover.

THE END.

Buy Books Online from

www.Booksophile.com

Explore our collection of books written in various languages and uncommon topics from different parts of the world, including history, art and culture, poems, autobiography and bibliographies, cooking, action & adventure, world war, fiction, science, and law.

Add to your bookshelf or gift to another lover of books - first editions of some of the most celebrated books ever published. From classic literature to bestsellers, you will find many first editions that were presumed to be out-of-print.

Free shipping globally for orders worth US$ 100.00.

Use code "Shop_10" to avail additional 10% on first order.

Visit today
www.booksophile.com

Lightning Source UK Ltd.
Milton Keynes UK
UKHW040636020323
417918UK00004B/154